Willie
Rum Running Queen

Based on the true story of Willie Carter Sharpe

Louella Bryant

Black Rose Writing | Texas

ISBN: 978-1-68513-554-6
PUBLISHED BY BLACK ROSE WRITING
www.blackrosewriting.com

Printed in the United States of America
Suggested Retail Price (SRP) $19.95

Willie—Rum Running Queen is printed in Book Antiqua

Praise for
Willie – Rum Running Queen

"Bryant's attention to detail is superb. She has captured a wonderful nostalgic spirit and the tension that exists within the novel's local community."
–Broo Doherty, DHH Literary Agency

"Bryant's passionate storytelling will captivate readers and bring a fresh perspective on a time of upheaval that reverberates in the twenty-first century."
–Jacquelyn Tuxill, author of *Whispers from the Valley of the Yak*

"Bryant is masterful at finding great true stories and bringing them to life."
–Sylvester Monroe, author of *Brothers: Black and Poor*

"In the first pages of *Willie – Rum Running Queen*, I could smell the broken earth, hear the sound of the tractor, and know the compelling characters who would become friends. This book is a hard and fruitful journey you will want to take. Every step was a pleasure."
–Scott Hammond, author of *Finding Asher*

"Willie's story is a reminder that what we want isn't always what we need. Well told and a joy to read."
–Elliott D. Light, author of *Throwaways and The Jackson River Bridge*

"Louella Bryant's character Willie roars through life in rural Virginia with courage and passion. During Prohibition she is devoted to fast bootlegging cars, lovemaking, and outwitting the law. Yet despite Willie's penchant for leaving the police in the dust, readers will identify with Willie as she struggles with heartache and setbacks."
–Joan Donaldson, author of *On Viney's Mountain*, winner of the Friends of American Writers Outstanding YA Novel for 2010

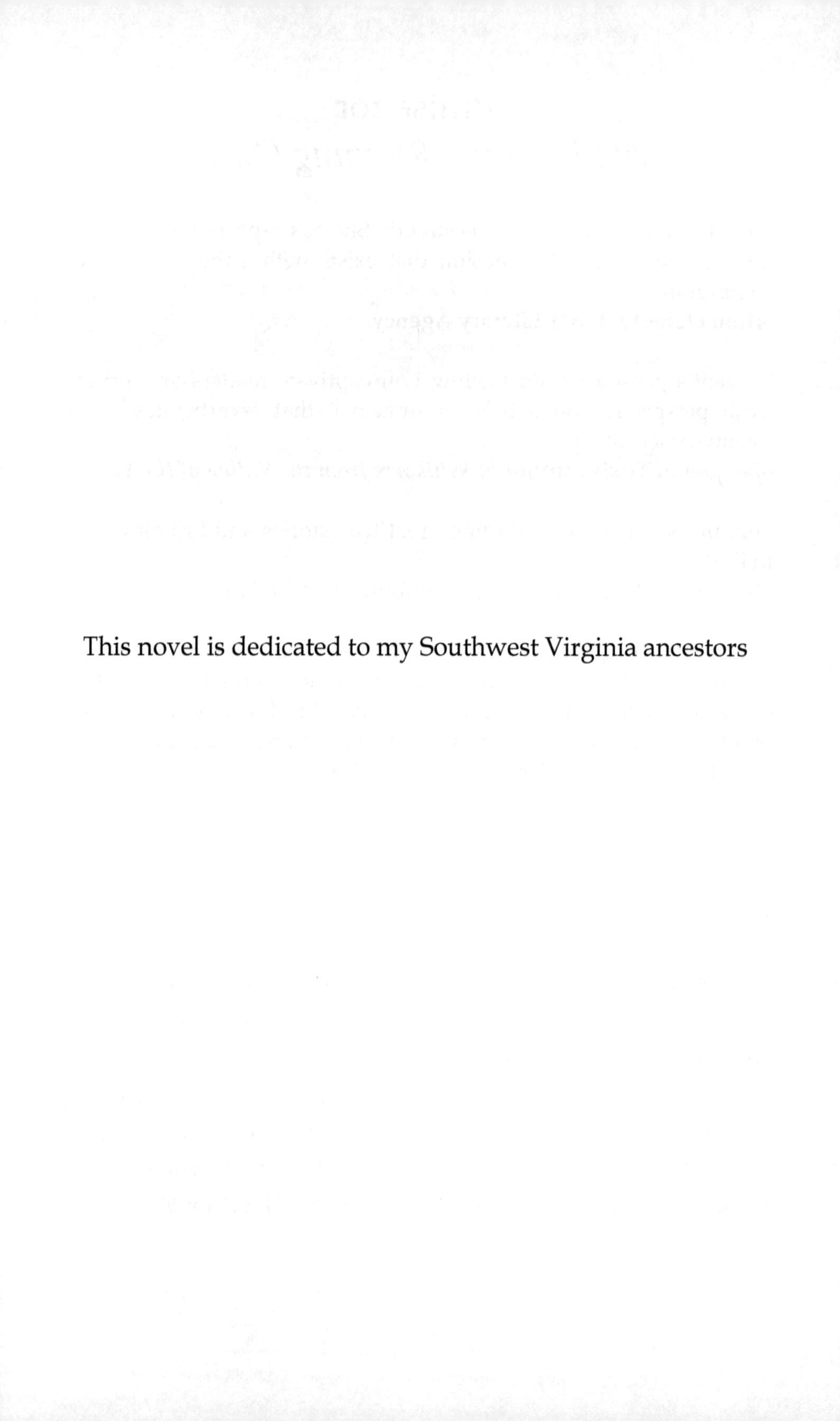

This novel is dedicated to my Southwest Virginia ancestors

Willie
Rum Running Queen

Based on the true story of Virginia bootleg whiskey runner,
Willie Carter Sharpe.

Jimmy ~ 1936

Willie May Collins—that's the name my sister was given at her birth in 1903. Our mother May—as she liked us to call her—wanted Wilhelmina written on the birth certificate, but Pop said Willie was good enough. He wanted a boy as his firstborn. Not to say he was disappointed, though. A girl could work as hard as a boy. He learned that from growing up on a farm with sisters who could handle a team of horses as well as any fellow. Willie grew to do a man's work and when she was a teenager, she understood engines better than most men.

By the time she was famous, if that's what you want to call it, my sister was going by Willie Carter Sharpe, which is how most folks knew her. I'm younger than Willie by four years and throughout my life I've held my sister in high regard. There's always been something setting her apart from most gals in the county, a type of knowing—not school learning but a knowing that comes from beyond books. It's hard to explain, but you'll get the picture when you hear Willie's story.

Willie and I were as close as two cubs in a den until she left to forge out on her own. On her visits to the farm, she spun stories about making big money driving fast cars. I'd hardly recognize her those times, pulling up to our dilapidated farmhouse in a flashy new car wearing silk dresses instead of the dungarees I was used to seeing her in. When we hadn't seen her in a spell, I followed her like most others through the newspaper and gossip. Seems everybody wanted to talk about my sister and what she came to be called—Queen of the Roanoke Rum Runners.

It's funny, though—I don't know why they called her that. From what I know, rum is made from sugarcane. Moonshine whiskey comes from corn, rye, and barley. Rum is dark, but moonshine is clear as glass. Whereas rum is sweet, moonshine liquor burns with its bitterness. Rum comes from Cuba and Virginia whiskey comes from our own back yards.

As far as Willie and her role in running moonshine, she'll tell it herself. Her recollection—and mine, if you want the truth—might be a bit fuzzy after all these years. Willie and I are kin with the same blood running through our veins. We have a bond, I guess you'd say, although our paths went different directions. But you don't need to know so much about me. I'll help her tell it, but this here's Willie's tale. So here goes.

1.
Junebug, 1918

Southwest Virginia is like nowhere else on earth. The humidity is so heavy I think about how a fish senses an angler's bait underwater. I am a fish with legs and arms swimming through air so moist you can see it rippling.

Everywhere you go in these hills there is the close or distant sound of a train. The whistle blasts an alert, then the rumble of metal wheels on metal tracks, the screech of hot metal laboring under the weight of coal or lumber or livestock, the metal odor of oil like a cast iron frying pan melting hog fat over an open fire. The smell of Pop's pocket watch was like that after he'd cleaned and oiled it, the gold watch that had been his father's and his father's father's and which he kept in a felt pouch because it was too rich to use on the farm where silage floated on the air and might foul the workings.

When I was young, the aromas of Southwest Virginia were so much a part of me they became indistinguishable from the smell of my own skin. There was pine and pawpaw, honeysuckle and loam, black soil composted from evergreen needles, oak leaves, bear and deer droppings, all damp with morning dew. Acrid smells, too, of paper mill, rayon and silk mills, the dry-nostril smell from kilns at the brickyard. The suffocating smell of coal smoke and wood-fire smoke rising from chimneys, and the sweet scent—always sweet—of a mash boiling corn into the liquor that lined men's pockets with money. By the food sellers at the market, little orange suns smelled of citrus mixed with the gamey reek of freshly butchered meat, the scent of earth clinging to unwashed potatoes, the sticky-sweet perfume of penny candies, their cheerful colors. And the ladies — their washed hair fragrance of a tropical island, the animal scents of their leather purses, and the dizzying milky bouquet of an underarm so close to the breast. The aromas of Southwest Virginia were like the earth itself exhaling.

Most of us in Floyd County stuck to our hills like ticks on a dog. Southwest Virginia was all we knew, and every single person settled here in Silver Ridge was Our People. Why in tarnation would you go anywhere else — that is, unless you had got a hankering like my sister Willie?

Our barn was close to the road for loading and unloading the farm truck, but the house was tucked back a ways so when Pop called you to get a move on, you could go out in your nightshirt without anybody noticing. And on a farm everything required you to high-tail it.

One sweltering July day, I was standing in the shade of the porch watching Willie apply her digging fork to the potato patch, her basket of spuds half full. She bent herself to the task and I knew better than to get in her way. When she straightened up and looked across the field, I could see she sensed something.

Pop was driving the steam tractor, its engine noise choking the life out of a peaceful day. The chimney belched smoke that reeked of burning coal, and the huffing machine dragged a sickle bar that cut the hay. I should have been out there tedding the hay into windrows so it would dry, and I meant to go. Honest I did. But Lord, it was hot. I wanted to peel out of my overalls — maybe even peel off my skin. When Willie finished digging those potatoes, we might catch a ride up to Stiles Falls for a swim. A day like this, lots of folks would be having the same idea.

In the distance, the Blue Ridge Mountains formed a hazy fringe at the horizon. Pop—Jim Collins as he was known in the county—idled the tractor, lifted his sweat-stained fedora, and wiped his forehead with his shirtsleeve. His face was leathery from the sun, and I thought he looked older than his forty years.

"Anything the matter, Pop?" Willie hollered.

Pop didn't answer. He spoke only when absolutely necessary. Even from the porch I could see a tree limb stuck in the tractor's wheel spokes. Pop hopped down and inspected the problem.

"You set the brake?" Willie called, her voice lost under the engine's growl.

The bough must have come from the apple tree at the south edge of the field, the only patch of shade on the cleared land. The tree made it harder to plow the field, but in the fall May cooked the fruit into a rich, sweet apple butter and pressed the drops into a decent cider that Pop hardened over the winter. I was glad he hadn't cut the tree down. Getting the limb out should have been an easy fix. Why bother with the brake if the job needed only a few seconds?

The steel wheels were as tall as I was, the rim a foot wide with brawn enough to support the tractor that weighed every bit of ten tons. More than a baker's dozen of spokes were welded to the rim, all of them placed barely wide enough apart for a man to stick in an arm to dislodge something like a tree branch.

I knew that steam built up if the engine idled too long. Some men in the county had red patches of skin where they'd been burned when they got too close to the engine casing. Pop stayed clear, but he had to get that branch out of the spokes.

Willie dropped her digging fork in the dirt and started toward the tractor.

"I'll get that, Pop," she called but if he heard her, he didn't let on.

Pop was wrestling with the black branch, big around as a full-grown cottonmouth. Leaning against the wheel, he pressed his forearm through the spokes to better reach the piece of wood. He couldn't have expected steam to burp from the tractor's chimney. Couldn't have expected the mechanism to lurch forward, the huge wheel to rotate. And for damn sight sure he couldn't have expected his arm to lurch with it, bending his elbow the wrong way and dragging him several yards.

When I heard him cry out, Willie was halfway across the farmyard, her pigtails flapping against her shoulders and her bare feet slapping dust out of the ground. Her old straw panama had slipped down behind her, the chin string holding it around her neck. She ran so fast I couldn't have counted to twenty and she was already at the tractor. Jumping atop the machine, she jerked the gearshift lever, gears grinding, and shut down the engine. It had taken an hour for Pop to build up a head of steam before the tractor was ready to go to work, but no one would be working the field the rest of this day.

She leaped from the tractor and reached to support Pop, who looked as though he'd fainted.

"Fetch the handsaw, Junebug!" she yelled.

For one split second I thought she intended to saw off Pop's arm to get him loose. Then I remembered the offending apple tree branch and whirled around to find the saw.

May must have heard him yell. She burst onto the porch, the screen door slapping shut behind her.

"What in heaven's name —" Her hand shielding her eyes, she looked at the tractor and shouted, "Oh, Lord." Before I reached the barn, she had one arm around a bundle of towels and the other holding her skirt above her knees and was running toward the tractor.

The saw hung inside the barn door, and I snatched it down so quick it bent the nail. I don't remember getting from the barn to the tractor. All I could recall was blood and a broken bone sticking through the skin of Pop's arm. He came to and moaned.

"Be still as you can, now," Willie said.

While May held his arm in place, I sawed as much of the tree limb as I could get to and pushed the rest through the wheel and under the tractor. Once the wood was out of the way, I watched Willie set her mind on bending the metal spokes apart. I mightn't have believed it if I hadn't seen it—a fifteen-year-old girl with that kind of strength.

May extracted the arm from the wheel, laid Pop on the ground, and tied towels around the injury. Then without looking up, she said, "Willie, take the truck and get the doc. Can't risk jostling him around in the back to get him to the hospital in Salem. And be quick about it." She shifted her eyes to me. "Junebug, help me get him to the house."

My official name, James Collins Junior, raised the question of what I should go by. I didn't like being tagged with the name Junior, so Willie took to calling me Junebug. She had her way of doing things, along with a short fuse, and it was not wise to argue with her. Junebug would have to be all right.

May and I half dragged my father to the porch and laid him on the divan. She tightened the towels around his arm to hold in the blood. He had passed out and there wasn't much more I could do, so I said, "I'm going with Willie."

My sister had never driven the old farm truck as far as I knew, but she had ridden with Pop enough times to understand its operation.

"Get in and pull out the choke," she ordered.

"The wagon might be faster," I offered.

"Don't be a fool—it'd take minutes to harness up the team, minutes we don't have. Besides, the Ford's got twenty horses under the hood and four cylinders."

I don't know how Willie understood so much about engines. I'd watched her tinker with the parts, and maybe she did some studying on her own, too. My interest was more along the lines of a game of kick the can.

"Keep her in neutral and pray the pistons catch when I crank the handle," Willie said. Through the windshield I could see her pigtails bouncing as she turned the crank. Within seconds, the engine ground to life.

"Tap on the gas pedal, Junebug."

When my bare foot bore down on the pedal, the grind turned to a growl. Willie climbed behind the wheel.

Old Betsy had three gears—down, over and up, and down to the right. I'd seen Pop get the four cylinders to churn out fifteen miles an hour, but I figured Willie could do better.

She shifted into first, the gear rattling its protest, and let up on the clutch. The truck jerked forward, nearly bucking me out of my seat.

"C'mon girl. C'mon. C'mon," Willie muttered. Betsy kicked up dirt, and she shifted into second. When we got to the road, she yanked the shift rod into third and pushed the gas pedal to the floor, driving as if her life—and our father's—depended on it. Even when she twisted the truck around sharp curves hellbent for the doctor, I wasn't afraid. Sitting beside Willie, I wasn't afraid of anything.

· · ·

When Willie got us back to the farm with Doc Brewster, May had wrapped a clean cloth around the injured arm and, from the sticky smell, had poured shine into him. He had come to, lips locked between his teeth, and stared out at the field like he was shellshocked.

I didn't see much blood, so May must have staunched it with a piece of torn sheet. Doc said to get him inside because any dust might lead to infection and he'd surely lose the arm. What a strange word, lose—as if he'd misplace it. Pop knew the exact location of everything on the farm, including in the cupboards of May's kitchen. He'd never lost anything as far as I knew. But I reckoned Doc meant he'd saw off the arm like I'd heard they did to wounded soldiers during the Civil War.

"Do whatever you've got to do," Willie said, "but don't take his arm." She bored into Doc's eyes with her own green torches. "He'd rather die."

When a horse broke a leg stepping into a gopher hole, it had to be shot. But no one was going to shoot Pop if I had anything to say about it.

Doc Brewster helped Willie and May get him to the bed. They set him down and swung up his feet, and Doc opened the black leather bag he had brought.

"Willie," he said, "crack a dozen egg whites into a pail with some vinegar, and grate in a potato and half a cup of wheat flour." He cast his eyes toward May. "You get some clean linen and soak it in the mixture."

May's mouth quivered. She smoothed her apron over her skirt. "I shouldn't leave him," she said.

Doc offered her a friendly smile. "I'll take good care of him, May. Once I get the bone set, the poultice should stem any infection and the linen will stiffen into a temporary splint until I come back to check on him." He pointed to his bag. "Then I'll cast the arm in plaster of Paris until the bones fuse."

Resigning herself to the doctor's medical authority, May gave him a nod and retreated to the linen closet.

Doc Brewster lifted a brown bottle from his bag and poured sweet-smelling liquid onto a cloth.

"Junebug," he said, holding the cloth toward me, "put this over your father's nose and mouth but try not to breathe it in — it's ether." Examining the crooked arm, he said, "But even when he's out, you'll have to keep him still while I set the bone."

He used his fingertips to unfold May's cloth. I could see what looked like a splintered stick, shiny red in the late morning light coming through the window. The broken bone stuck a couple of inches through a ragged hole in the flesh. It felt wrong to witness a thing inside him, a glimpse of the skeleton that held together the sinew and muscle I'd depended on all my life. It was as if that tractor had disgraced him, stripping him naked and robbing him of his dignity.

Whether because of the shard of bone or the ether, my head started swimming and I staggered backward.

"Junebug," the doctor said, "you've got to hold…."

"You go on out and get some air." Willie had come up behind me. She snatched the cloth from my shaking hand. "I'll take over here."

Pop's eyes were wild before she pressed the cloth to his face, and slowly I watched his lids close. I should have felt ashamed I wasn't up to Doc's task, but truth be told, I was relieved — relieved and grateful for a sister who regarded a broken bone the same way she did a faulty piston. The body was just another machine that needed fixing, and if Doc Brewster hadn't come, I'd bet on Willie May Collins to fix up Pop her own self.

2.
Willie

A week later, Junebug was sitting on the porch whittling at a piece of hemlock when I came up the steps, paying no mind to the splintered pine under my bare feet. In the heat, strands of my hair had come loose from my pigtails and I felt them curling around my face.

"Hey, Willie," Junebug said.

"Hey. Pop feeling any better?"

"Have to ask him."

Pop was sitting up in a rocker, his arm in a sling. I pulled up a milk stool and sat at his knee. He was staring at the field, then raised his eyes to the sky.

"Mares tail clouds," he said. "Storm's coming in a day or two. Got to get that hay in."

"I'll do it," I said.

"You'd better harness up the horses."

"I can handle the tractor, Pop." I'd helped him get the steam going most every day and even rode on the tractor with him a few times. I had a knack with machinery even from the days we plowed the fields with horses, cleaning dirt from the metal after every use and coating the teeth with oil to keep rust off. In the best of conditions, horses could plow only three acres a day if there were no rocks in the way. A steam tractor could go all day once it was primed. And you didn't have to feed it hay or get it shod.

"That tractor's got a bad attitude. A horse bites you, you can bite it back," Pop said.

"It'll go easier with the tractor," I insisted. "I can manage it."

He worked his mouth, considering my proposal. In no position to argue, he said, "You've got to tote wood to start the fire and fill the basin with water to get up a head of steam."

"I know," I said.

"It'll take all of an hour, so best get started." Pop jerked his head toward the screen door leading into the parlor. "Bring me a jar of that shine first."

I knew what Pop needed. When it came to liquor, Appalachians felt entitled to drink what they produced from the corn and rye they'd grown in their own fields and made from stills forged with their own hands. Aging whiskey in barrels to mellow the flavor took up too much space in the barn so if you were going to drink it, you had to get used to the burn. Moonshine was a way of life in the Blue Ridge.

I scrabbled into the house, the screen door slapping my behind to keep it from slamming shut, more out of habit than thoughtfulness. I got a jelly jar from the cupboard and poured in the clear liquid from a jug. Most everyone in Floyd County made moonshine, and Pop was no exception. Corn whiskey, some called it because of the ingredients—corn, yeast, and spring water. Some distillers added barley and sugar, but Pop said his corn was sweet enough. He didn't sell much of it, which kept him out of the clink, and the Feds cut him a wide swath. Wasn't making enough moonshine to worry them with. I hadn't yet developed a taste for whiskey unless I mixed in some damson plum juice. Then a couple sips and I was ready to hit the hay and sleep like the dead.

I brought the jar out to the porch and handed it to Pop.

"Ease down gentle on the pedal," he said. "Tractor's got a kick worse'n a mule."

I took long strides to the tractor trying to act nonchalant, a word I'd picked up somewhere. It meant being casual, not concerned. Pop had never trusted me alone with the steam tractor before. And he was mighty proud of that machinery. Spent a whole season in hay for it and still making payments. In my point of view, steam tractors were good for breaking up soil, but they were so heavy they sank down into plowed fields. Horses had a delicate step, and you could reason with them. But Pop set his mark on me — we both favored modern gadgets over pure flesh and muscle.

I brought the wood for the firebox, enough to steam water for a couple hours, and made three trips from the pump carrying a full pail in each hand. While the water heated, I climbed onto the tractor. There was no seat, so I stood behind the hissing and spitting engine like driving a boisterous chariot. The platform was hot and I shifted from one bare foot to the other, one hand on the steering wheel and the other on the brake. When finally I pushed the gear lever, the apparatus lurched forward and died.

"Hells bells." I slapped the steering wheel and worked at starting it again only to have it pitch forward and quit.

Pop hobbled toward the tractor carrying an old pair of boots under his good arm.

"Hold on there." He held the boots up to me. The laces were broken, the sole separating. "These'll give you better traction. Wore out, but they ought ta do."

"Your old boots?" I blinked. Neither Junebug nor I owned a pair of warm-weather shoes. How many times had we bandaged slices in our feet and rubbed liniment onto bruises caused by stones? I liked the feel of the earth under me, almost as if I had sprouted up from the rich Virginia soil itself. But when it came to engines, I reckoned Pop had a point.

I accepted the boots and jammed my feet into them. Lifting up one foot and then the other, I laughed. "Feet don't know what to think," I said.

A grin split Pop's face. "Feet should think about getting that hay in." He shook a finger at me. "And don't try to set no speed record. This fella might get up to three miles per hour with a wind behind him, but you work him hard, the better he'll like it."

When he tossed a quick look to Junebug biting his fingernails on the porch, I reckoned Pop thought of the tractor as a "fella" because his only son preferred playing games and woolgathering to working hard.

I eased the tractor forward, and it found its ground. We were in business.

Pop stood beside the field and watched, his good hand twitching as if he were operating the machine himself. From the corner of my eye I saw May come onto the porch and peer at her daughter aboard the monstrosity. May believed you couldn't beat a team of horses when it came to farm work. But the kitchen was her domain—and the vegetable garden—and she held her tongue rather than criticize Pop's field management. She shielded her eyes with one hand and a dishtowel dangled from the other.

She came down the steps and stood by Pop. I couldn't hear her exact words over the sputter of the machine, but I knew what she was saying. Those two had had conversations along the same lines before.

"You'd think she was born to that machine," May would say.

"She'll make a good farm wife one of these days," Pop would answer.

"I was hoping for something more for her." May again, always wishing for more than farming for her children—the same something more she had wished for herself before she fell in love with a farmer.

Holding the tractor in a straight line, I watched Pop lay his good arm around her shoulders. "Nothing finer than this life, and you know it," he would tell her.

May slapped his thigh with the dishtowel. What she always said was, "We'll see about that, Mr. Collins."

I liked when they sparred like that, especially when she called him "Mr. Collins," which I thought affectionate and respectful.

When I reached the edge of the field, I made a neat turn on the tractor. Up so high on the metal Goliath I was on top of the world, in control. There was nothing I couldn't do and no one to stop me from doing it.

•   •   •

After that, driving the farm truck fell to me. Junebug generally walked from school, but I had finished my chores—except for kitchen work, which I avoided like poison oak. May gave me dispensation because not only did I have a tendency to nick my knuckles on the washboard and hang the dripping clothes on the line so close together they never dried even in the heat of Virginia sun, but I left bits of food in the pots so that May had to scrub them a second time. No amount of scolding from May improved my domestic efforts, and she thought it better to send me off in the truck to get Junebug.

The farm truck had a wide wheel base and wooden rails on the flatbed to hold bales of hay in place. I had studied the engine and found I could get more clout than Pop ever had by pulling out the sparkplugs and cleaning them. I figured they'd run hotter if they were clean but not so hot as to burn off the lubricant. The engine needed more compression, and I was trying to figure out a way to get more air into the carburetor.

Junebug once asked me, "How do you know about the workings of a gasoline engine?"

I shrugged. "Makes sense if you ponder it long enough." Trouble with Junebug was he couldn't ponder anything for very long before having to scoot off somewhere.

The schoolhouse was nearly five miles up the road, a slight incline to which the farm truck objected. I saw Junebug at the top of the hill and shifted into second gear. He was walking at a slight stagger, bumping shoulders with a pretty dark-haired girl. I let off the gas and pressed the brake pedal.

"Hop in, Junebug," I said.

He hesitated and blinked at the girl.

"You want a ride, too, honey?" I asked her.

Junebug had mentioned this girl before—Dottie was her name. She looked at the truck as if she'd never seen a motorized vehicle before. I would not have been surprised. Most farmers still used horses to pull plows and wagons, working them until they fell over and died, a boon for getting fresh meat on the table.

The girl shook her brown curls.

Junebug hauled himself onto the bench—cracked brown leather—waved to Dottie, and stared out the window at a cornfield, stalks dry in this late autumn.

When we were out of earshot, he groused, "Why'd you hafta come get me for anyway?"

"Pop needs you to fix that fence before dark."

It was an excuse—a quick think on my part. My brother knew full well I'd find any reason to drive.

"Why can't you fix the damn fence?"

His oath didn't faze me. I loved my brother.

"You got to learn to do things on the farm, Junie. I'm not gonna be here forever."

"Where you going?"

I chewed my lip before I answered. "Thinking I'll get me a job."

I had run down my list of skills, which didn't amount to much. Hoeing potatoes. Weeding turnips, thinning carrots. And driving. But I was strong and smart, and even with only a sixth-grade education, I could learn to do anything. Anything but housework, that was.

"A job? Where at?" he asked.

"Don't rightly know yet."

"You ain't gonna move into town, are you, Willie?"

"Naw. Nothing'll change, Junebug."

I'd been wanting change, craving it. But Pop still had some healing to do, and he needed me. Soon enough I might find employment in Silver Ridge or over to Christiansburg. Maybe even all the way up in Roanoke.

"I oughta give up going to that school and work for Pop," Junebug said. "Don't learn nothing worth anything anyway."

"School's good for you, boy."

"You quit—"

"Never mind what I did. Look, if I'd stayed in school, I might have worked in a dress shop and bought some fancy duds. Shoes, too. I'da bought both of us some shoes."

I looked at Junebug's feet caked with dirt. "What kind of girl would go for a boy with callouses on his toes from stumbling over rocks? You stay in that school as long as you can, you hear?"

Just as I took my eyes off his feet and looked through the windshield, I saw the truck had drifted to the middle of the road and a loaded hay wagon was coming headlong toward us.

"Look out, Willie!" Junebug yelled.

I downshifted and swerved into the field on the right, running down tobacco plants for which I'd surely get an earful—unless I could get up to the road and hightail it down the hill.

"Hold tight, Junebug," I said.

He grabbed the dashboard as we careened through the corn stubs.

I whooped and yelled "Hot damn!"

When we were well clear of the wagon, I barreled the truck back onto the dirt road, dust swirling up behind us like a small tornado.

Junebug looked at me and shook his head. "Willie, I swear—you must be about the best driver in the whole of Floyd county."

I beamed at him. "You better believe it," I said.

· · ·

"Take your seat, Willie," May said. "I'll serve us tonight.

"Something special going on?" Junebug asked.

"Might be," May said.

The table was of heavy oak and had belonged to our grandmother. Rarely had Pop bought anything new except for farm equipment. Inside the house, we made do. But I liked the table with its dents and watermarks, its four sturdy legs. Besides wood chairs, the table was the only furniture in the kitchen and served for preparing meals, eating meals, filling canning jars with beet pickles and pickled eggs, green beans and apple butter, and for writing letters and paying bills.

"What've you got on tonight's menu, May?" Pop asked. His arm was no longer in a sling, but it hung at an odd angle. Occasionally he rubbed his elbow, but his hands seemed to work all right.

I wore my auburn hair in pigtails secured with string, but I had scrubbed up for supper, brushed dirt from my trousers and buttoned up a clean shirt, collar open, sleeves rolled to the elbows. I liked being comfortable. The one skirt I owned had hung on a peg since I couldn't remember when. Junebug's christening maybe. Trousers were more practical—warmer, too, for winters in Silver Ridge. It wasn't unusual to get a couple feet of snow up on Buffalo Mountain, and Silver Ridge was only a thousand feet lower. Often snow stayed in the fields for the entire winter and we all shivered in front of the fire, even when we were wrapped in woolens. Not long after dark we took to bed and snuggled under May's hand-stitched quilts. I counted on the city having insulation and more efficient heat.

"Elbows off the table," May said. Junebug scowled. We weren't upper class, but May insisted on practicing manners as if we were. Junebug slid his elbows off but leaned his forearms against the table edge.

"Let us bow our heads," Pop said, and he led with his usual short but sweet grace. "Bless us, Oh Lord, and these thy gifts which we are about to receive."

"Amen," May pronounced, her signal to dig in with as much restraint as a farm family could manage.

I cleared my throat, announcing I was about to speak. "Pop, you're back to handling the tractor real good," I said, passing the mashed potatoes to Junebug.

"Doc Brewster fixed me up," he said. "A fine man."

"Right. And Jimmy's a big help around here." My brother had turned twelve, and it was time his family started calling him by his real name. Jim Collins, Junior. I called him Jimmy so as not to confuse him with our father.

Pop was helping himself to the bowl of winter squash. He stopped the spoon in midair and looked at me.

"Something on your mind, Willie?" He knew his daughter pretty well.

"She's got herself a job," Jimmy blurted.

Pop planted an elbow on the table, for which May would never scold him, and balled his hand into a soft fist. I liked that pose. There was an elegance about it, as if he was some hotshot southern gentleman lording over his brood.

"Her job's right here on the farm," he said.

"Where will you be working, Willie May?" Our mother had married Pop when she was still a teenager. I always thought she held some resentment about missing out on bettering herself or at least settling for more than the drudgery of a farmer's wife.

"Tobacco factory." I spoke to my plate. "Pay's not much to sing about, but it's a start. I've got to get my foot in somewhere."

"You plan to pick tobacco?" Pop said. "Better to work here on the farm."

"Not picking it, no. I can make a dollar a day rolling cigarettes. Nothing to it."

I wanted to be clear I was not going to be doing field work. I had bigger ideas for myself.

"You get them cigarettes for free?" Jimmy asked.

"You don't need any cigarettes, Jimmy," I said. "Don't get started smoking. You'll be coughing and wheezing before you're twenty."

Truth was, no one in our family smoked except Pop when he could lay hands on tobacco for his pipe. Most of the time he chewed on the stem, pretending.

"I can do my chores in the morning and work the afternoon shift at the factory," I said. I had already made the arrangements and gotten agreement from the foreman.

"Junebug—Jimmy—can do some chores after school," May said. "We'll manage."

"Only if she brings home some cigarettes," he said.

I had never spoken harshly to my brother. We were allies, and I liked having him on my side.

"I'll be working for cold, hard cash, Jimmy. I'll buy you anything you want—except cigarettes."

"I don't like it," Pop said.

"Let the girl grow up, Jim," May said. "She's nearly sixteen. You can't expect her to stay on the farm forever."

Pop regarded his potatoes. I had never heard him use a stern tone with May, as far as I could remember. Not even a word to challenge her. Her parents had a nice house and a maid to clean and cook. Gramps had nearly disowned her for marrying beneath her. May probably hoped to convince her new husband to rise above digging in the soil. But Pop knew only one way to live—and cared only for that one livelihood—nurturing plants from the ground, tending livestock, coaxing machinery into compliance. But out of love our mother had bent her back to the hard task of farm wifery. I knew I would come out a winner on the issue of her only daughter bettering herself.

I scooted from my chair and kissed him on the cheek. "Thanks, Pop!"

Pop met May's eyes. May looked at her plate and quickly wiped her mouth.

3.
Jimmy—1920

Didn't my sister know smoking a fag was a way to let off stress—stresses like going to school and doing farm chores? I tried to tell her puffing on a cigarette was respectable, especially since I was fourteen now, but she said she was looking out for my best interests. I suspected she smoked now and then herself, but she wouldn't let on.

Willie moving away a few months ago got me thinking about the wider world. I read the evening paper and kept my ears open to talk in town. This past winter the WCTU—a group of women sick to death of their husbands' drinking—convinced lawmakers to pass an act outlawing alcohol across the country. Even though President Wilson tried to veto the bill, the Eighteenth Amendment passed and the making, sale, transport, delivery, and possession of alcohol was against the law. In case the desperate-to-drink tried to cross the border, up north in Canada the law put a limit on the alcohol in their drinks. Drinks were so weak a fellow would have to pour a lot of Canadian beer down his gullet to get staggering drunk. If Canadian farmers were anything like in Virginia, they were probably making their own hooch in the woods and drinking it on the sly.

As for Willie, she was good at rolling cigarettes, so good that after a week boredom set in. I knew Willie didn't take to boredom. You'll see what I mean if you'll be patient.

4.

Willie

I cut my hair to the chin in the style I'd seen in a fashion magazine. Lois, my new friend at the factory, showed me the pictures on our lunch break. Lois was a year younger than I was and aspired to be a model once she saved enough to get up to New York. I squinted at her when she told me that. I didn't think she looked anything like the women in the magazine — she was short and stubby and had an overbite that made her look like a turtle. Nothing wrong with having dreams, though. I had a few of my own, in fact. Rolling cigarettes was the first step. I'd figure out the next step when the time was right.

Late one morning at the factory I looked at Lois across the rolling table.

"How many you rolled, Lo?" I asked.

Lois frowned at the box next to her. "A thousand, I reckon."

"That ain't but fifty-five cents." I grabbed a handful of cigarettes from my own box and shoved them toward her. "Here. That'll buy you a pound of bacon."

"Willie, you're a doll," Lois said.

I waved her off. "Aw, I'm a sap and you know it."

Lois helped support a houseful of brothers and sisters. I was lucky that way. Pop was a dirt farmer, but he did well enough by his family, and he hadn't asked me for a nickel.

On our breaks, we gathered in the lunchroom for a round of cards — poker usually.

"You up for a game, Lo?" I asked.

"Sure," Lois said. "I've got to win back what you took off me yesterday."

"Fat chance, lady." Actually, once in a while I let Lois win a hand to even the score. I didn't mind being generous, especially when she didn't notice.

When we entered the lunchroom, Juanita and Ethel were already seated at the wide wood table, the top marked with scars from years of tough tobacco workers having their lunch and taking out their frustrations. I dropped into an empty chair and put my feet on the tabletop. My new pair of boots actually fit me, bought with my first paycheck. Lois put a bottle in front of me.

"Here's a Dr. Pepper for you, Willie." There was a lift-top cooler in the back, and the company let us help ourselves to as much soda pop as we wanted. "I hope it brings you the worst of luck."

I sat up and started dealing out a round of cards. "Don't need luck. I've got skill — and a bit of this." I pulled a flask out of my pocket, bit the cork from the lid, and poured some into my bottle.

"Where'd you get that?" Juanita asked.

"This panther juice? It's made in my Pop's own still."

"Your daddy makes moonshine?"

"You should know that, Nita — your daddy makes it, too."

Lois studied the fan of cards in her hand, ignoring the conversation. "I'll take two." She laid two cards facedown, and I dealt her a couple more in the easy motion I'd acquired from our daily breaks playing cards.

"Not my daddy," Juanita said. "He's a preacher." Juanita was tall and beanpole thin with teeth so bucked she couldn't get her lips together to say the word preacher.

"How do you think your preacher papa keeps you in shoes when the congregation pays him in eggs and sausage?" Lois said. "He's making it, all right — "

"He's just not talking about it," Ethel said, laying down her cards. "I fold."

"Here, Nita." I pushed the flask toward Juanita. "Have a splash of mother's milk."

Lois slapped down her card hand, face up. "Yeah, you splash while I clean up this table." A straight, all diamonds. She raked coins from the tabletop with her arms.

"I've had about enough of this," I said.

"Don't you want to play anymore, Willie?" Ethel asked.

"I mean I've had enough of this factory work. I'm giving my notice tomorrow."

"What're you going to do?" Juanita asked.

"I hear they're hiring at the five and dime in Roanoke," Lois said. "That would be a proper job. You'd meet a decent sort there."

"Hey, I'm decent," Juanita protested. She pulled a compact from her purse and wiped pinkish powder on her nose, pulling her upper lip down over her horse teeth.

Lois lifted the flask. "Well, then, when you get home you better get down on your knees and ask your decent preacher daddy to forgive you for drinking this moonshine."

"Ha!" I laughed while I shuffled the cards. "He's probably loaded hisself."

"If it works out," Lois said, "there's a rooming house down a short way from the dime store. Maybe you and me could share a room there, Willie."

"I'll drink to that." I lifted my Dr Pepper and clinked with Lois's. "Okay, one more hand and then somebody better help me get fixed up for that five and dime."

5.
Jimmy — 1920

Growing up on a farm, I learned at a young age about the desire to mate. I was almost fifteen when a girl — most of a woman at sixteen — taught me you don't go at it like the bull at the heifer. My sweetheart Dottie didn't know about Lila, and I planned to keep it that way. Lila was taller than I was and even though she had quit school, she hung out there when her father didn't need her on the farm. One day she asked me to help her get some hay bales into the loft of their barn. She had some lessons to teach me I couldn't learn in school, she said.

A stallion courts the mare by nosing around her hind end to get her in the mood, and even then she has to be in heat. But human beings are different. A fella's got to impress a gal somehow. Like how a male bird attracts the lady of his desires with his colorful plumage or a sweet song or even a nimble dance. I might have flexed some muscles around Lila. Or maybe it was my ignorance about what I was expected to do. Some females like to be in the driver's seat, and Lila was one of them.

"Whatcha got in them overalls, Jimmy?" she asked once we were in the hayloft.

Dumb as a stone, I said, "Nothing but a quartz crystal and a couple pennies." I wondered if she was looking to ask me for money.

"Let me see," she said. Before I could object, she unfastened the bib of my overalls and pulled them down. Well, you can imagine my embarrassment. But Lila wasn't finished. She leaned in close for a good long study of my male equipment, petting it, squeezing it in her fist, and even kissing it. Honestly, it took my breath away.

You won't be surprised I lost track of time in that loft until it was nearly dark and I had to run home barely in time for supper. When I sat down, May pulled a straw from my hair and asked what I'd been doing. Pop was pretty proud of me when I told him I was helping Lila with the hay. I helped her a few more times, but you don't need to know about that.

My sister liked to be in a different kind of driver's seat, and a gentleman named Floyd Carter had the equipment to offer her a temptation Willie was not able to resist.

6.
Willie – 1920

At the cigar counter, I opened a box and put it in the glass showcase. The store manager paid me by the hour, but I had to push smokes in order to keep the dime store job and business that day was slow.

A slender man strutted in wearing a light-colored suit on this warm day with a bow tie, of all things, at his neck. He looked to be in his twenties, a few years older than I was, and he sauntered toward the counter like a peacock with his tail feathers fanned out. A big shot, at least in his own imagination.

"Help you?" I asked. I put on my courtesy act hoping he might buy a few smokes.

"What're you putting out?" he said.

"I don't put out. I sell cigars." I had no patience for dandies. Did he want a cigar or didn't he?

The fellow gave me a half smile, the right side of his mouth twisting upward.

"Show me the best you've got."

I looked through the glass top of the showcase.

"You can get a Jenny Lind for ten cents. That's a popular brand." I hoped the popularity of the cigar would entice him.

"Do I look like I'd smoke a ten-cent cigar?"

Figuring he was an easy mark, I obliged him with an offer of the store's premium smokes.

"I don't know what you look like, mister, but I can sell you one of these Cubans for two dollars." I lifted out a box. The man picked up a cigar and held it under his nose. Apparently the aroma agreed with him because he pulled a cigar clipper from his pocket and clipped the tip.

"You got a light?" he said.

"Not until you pay for it. S.H. Hieronymus doesn't give out free samples." The customer's nerve rankled me. Was he a thief? I didn't think so—not dressed like he was.

He extracted a roll of money from another pocket, flipped off four ten-dollar bills, and tossed them on the counter.

"Wrap up the box."

I gathered the money trying not to raise an eyebrow and settled the bills in the cashbox. Then I reached for a box of matches, struck one straight down on the side of the box, and held it up toward the man's cigar. He took a puff and blew the smoke toward the ceiling.

"How old are you anyway?"

I stuck out my chin. "What's it to you?"

"You're a real bearcat, ain't you? I'll bet you're not more than eighteen." He held up his cigar and studied the burning end. "What time you finish up here?"

Was he asking me out? He wasn't half bad looking, and neither was the fat wad of bills I'd seen. I'd have to work years to save that kind of cash.

"Might be around five."

He put the box of cigars under his arm and saluted me with the lighted stogie.

"Five o'clock." He gave a subtle nod and squinted at me. "What'd you say your name was?"

I was tempted to give a false name, but it wouldn't take much even in a town the size of Roanoke to find out my real identity.

"Willie May," I said, not bothering to add my last name. If he was some sort of criminal, I wouldn't want him tracking down my family.

He turned to go and twisted his head before he reached the door.

"See you at five, Willie May."

Lois had watched the exchange from the cosmetic counter. She came up to me and slipped her hand inside my elbow.

"You know who that was, Willie?"

"Some drugstore cowboy with a lot of dough," I said.

Lois rolled her eyes through the storefront glass to the man getting into a late-model convertible. Then she leaned into me as if she had a big secret to tell.

"That's Floyd Carter. His daddy's the biggest bootlegger in the county," she said. "The Carters can buy and sell both of us. You better watch yourself and see that you don't get your behind in serious trouble."

"Yeah?" I said. "Then trouble better be driving a Super Six to catch me."

• • •

At quitting time, I clocked out to find Floyd out front in his shiny Buick, top down, engine idling, arm across the seat. He motioned me into the passenger's seat, not bothering to open the door for me. Not that I expected him to. I was used to doing for myself.

He shifted into gear and pressed easy on the gas, checking the rearview mirror as if he expected to be followed.

"Where'd you get such a nice jalopy?" I asked. I hadn't seen one like it in Roanoke.

"She's got sixty-one horsepower under the hood. You fancy her?" he said without answering my question.

"Can't tell 'til you let me drive her," I said.

His face screwed into a question. "You know how to drive?"

I had heard men at the dime store ridiculing women drivers. Slowpokes. Don't know how to handle the machinery. Can't keep the car on the road. There was no use arguing with them. For women, driving was useful and a good automobile could give a gal a shot of adrenaline. Why shouldn't women drive?

"Only one way to find out, mister," I said.

Floyd pulled the car over on a quiet stretch of road. When he got out I slid behind the wheel. While he climbed into the passenger side, I shifted into first and let off the clutch before he had the door closed.

"Better hang on," I said.

I floored the gas pedal and the engine roared. When I snapped a quick look at Floyd, his teeth were gritted in a forced smile. I had to admit the Buick was a world beyond anything I'd driven before. I tested it on a straightaway, burying the accelerator in the floorboard and fishtailing the rear end around a hairpin turn. The sixty-one horses galloped up a hill without complaint, and I pressed the gas pedal for the pure thrill of watching Floyd's eyes register fear. Farmhouses, barns, and cattle smeared into a blur as I picked up speed on a straightaway.

"Whoa now," Floyd grumbled. I laughed.

Finally, I brought the car to a squealing stop in front of the boarding house where Lois and I lived. When I looked at Floyd, his face was ghostly pale.

"I reckon you left a patch of rubber on the road," he said, catching his breath.

"You still want to know what I think?" I said.

"All right." His voice was less sure than earlier that afternoon.

"She handles pretty good." I got out and walked around the front of the car to the sidewalk. Floyd stepped out and grabbed my wrist.

"You want to know what I think?" he said.

I tossed my nose in the air. "You think you're a big shot."

He pulled me against his chest and kissed me hard on the mouth. I tasted stale tobacco on his breath.

"I *am* a big shot," he said. "And to show you how big, I'll be outside your dungeon of drudgery tomorrow, same time."

I broke loose and started up the walk to the boarding house. Before I reached the door, I turned toward him.

"We'll see about that," I said. "But thanks for the ride."

•　　•　　•

For the next month, Floyd showed up at quitting time and let me drive the Buick. Most days he had moved over to the passenger side so I could take the wheel when I came out of Hieronymus. I drove through small towns of Hanging Rock and Cave Spring. Once, all the way out to Stewartsville. On a Sunday I steered the Buick up to Potts Creek where my Aunt Emma lived in a one-story house with a porch all along the front. Buxom as a beach ball, Emma greeted us and would not hear of us leaving before she whipped up Sunday lunch and served it outside on the picnic table. When she brought out a pitcher of lemonade, Floyd added a dose of his own specialty, and we laughed and ate beside the gurgling brook.

One evening after work I found Floyd's car, gray top up in a soft drizzle of rain. He had parked by the curb in the same spot as before and was sitting in the driver's seat.

"You going to move over?" I said.

"You're not driving this afternoon, Willie," he said.

"Why not?"

He jerked his head toward the back seat. "Might be something for you there."

I spied a box, a pink one big enough to hold a curled up boa constrictor, with a blue ribbon tied around it. Floyd got out of the car and folded the seat forward so I could climb in.

"Go on," he said. "Open it."

I sat sideways on the seat and pulled off the ribbon.

"Does it bite?" I asked.

He gave a soft laugh. "Better watch your fingers."

I lifted the top. Inside, tissue paper whispered. No matter what was under the paper, no one had ever given me a gift wrapped in such a fashion.

"Is this some kind of trick?"

"More like a treat," Floyd said. "I don't waste dough on tricks."

Carefully I pulled away the paper expecting something to jump out. Instead, I found silk. Peach colored silk. I held up the material. Narrow shoulder straps and lace above the bust. A dropped waist like dresses in Lois's magazines. High fashion. And not from a secondhand store.

"What's this for?" I dared not take my eyes off the dress in case Floyd should scoop it up and have a big laugh at my gullibility.

"It's for you," he said.

I narrowed my eyes at him. "Floyd Carter, if you think this dress is going to buy you privileges—"

"Now hold on a minute, girl." He shook a finger at me. The windows were down and he stood in the sprinkle, the brim of his fedora shielding his face. "We're going dancing tonight. I'll pick you up at eight, and you better be wearing this frock." He tossed a ten-dollar bill in the box. "And find a pair of dancing shoes to match. Only thing tonight'll cost you is a fox trot around the dance floor."

"You trying to make a lady out of me, Floyd Carter?"

He snorted. "Why would I want to make a lady out of someone who's so much a woman?"

Lord, I thought, Lois was going to have to show me what a fox trot was. And how to pour myself into this awfully pretty dress.

•   •   •

"You have fun tonight?" Floyd said. He tottered while we walked from the Roanoke Park pavilion to the parking lot. Roanoke was dry, but Floyd had brought a flask of his father's juice and added some to our glasses of punch. I sipped one glass throughout the evening and lost count of how many Floyd had.

I let him put his hand around my waist to steady himself. It was the least I could do. The dress must have cost him twenty bucks and I felt like a million in it.

"Sure," I said. "I had a real good time." I meant it. Women looked at me with envy and men with interest on the verge of desire. What woman wouldn't puff up with that kind of attention?

He pushed his face close to mine. His breath was so sweet with liquor it nearly turned my stomach. "How's about you come to my house for a midnight toddy?" he said.

Arm around the waist was one thing, but I wasn't about to give Floyd free entrance into my panties—at least not yet.

"Not a chance," I said. "I'm beat."

He sighed. "All right then. Let me ask you this—what is it you want, Willie?"

I smirked. I'd been seeing Floyd for four months, but I hadn't made any commitment to him. What harm was there in telling him the truth? Worst case, he'd drop me and I'd be none the worse for wear.

"I want a nickel for every dime you've got."

Floyd laughed. "I might be able to make that happen."

But I wasn't finished. "And a fast car of my own."

"Can make that happen, too."

"How?"

Floyd took his time answering.

"Marry me," he said.

Floyd was jumping the gun, even if the Carters were the most powerful bootleg family in the county.

"Marry you?"

Floyd swiveled his head, searching the dark lot. "You see anyone else around here proposing marriage?"

I remembered what Lois had told me. The Carters get what they want, no questions asked. He'd already been married and divorced once. If Floyd wanted me, he'd have me one way or another.

"You could quit that five and dime job," he said. "Move out of the boarding house into a proper residence." He winked at me. "You'll have more luxury than you've ever dreamed of."

Did I love him? No—but did love really matter? If I could believe in destiny, it was destiny that brought Floyd into Hieronymus that day. And when it came to destiny, who was I to argue?

"Well, then," I said, "I guess as long as it's on my terms."

7.
Jimmy – 1922

My best dungarees didn't suit the occasion of my sister's wedding, so I stood in the back like a tramp who'd wandered in. May and Pop sat up front, my mother in a good dress that must've been a dozen years old. Being a farm wife, she was too busy to put on weight, and the dress still fit her. Pop had a necktie peeping over a buttoned-up vest. It was too hot for a jacket, but tell that to the Carters who suffered through the heat in suits. John Carter, I guess it was, wiped his forehead a few times with a neatly folded handkerchief, and the groom pulled at his collar.

I was going on sixteen now and still seeing Lila on the sly once in a while, although I figured Dottie was getting suspicious. Lila had taught me some tricks I was eager to try out with Dottie, but Dottie was holding out. Sometimes when we sparked I felt I might bust wide open, but I respected Dottie. She had a sense of honor. I wouldn't call what Lila and I did sparking, exactly. It was more like exploring. I was her uncharted territory, and she mapped me like a surveyor. I admit I did some surveying, too. You might say I was getting a degree in human geography – and I was getting A-plus in the course.

So there they were, Willie and Floyd standing before what must have been a justice of the peace, although I wasn't sure a marriage to Willie May Collins could stay peaceful for long. Knowing Willie, love was not the issue. Floyd could give her wings. Who cared if he hadn't even come out to the house to ask Pop for Willie's hand? I reckon old Floyd knew from the get-go Willie was going to be true to her own lights, no matter what Pop said. Reckon Pop knew it, too.

8.
Willie — 1922

Floyd had wanted a fancy wedding, but where was a nineteen-year-old gal from a dirt-farming family supposed to get a gown? I had saved some from my salary and bought myself a cream-colored suit — linen, since the ceremony was set for early August and bound to be hot. The suit and matching hat with a narrow rim twisting down over my right eye were fine enough for the Richmond Courthouse, a grand building that had survived a fire set by the Union army in the last days of the Civil War.

Floyd sent a driver to take me to the courthouse. When I arrived, he was standing in the shade of the portico. It must have been ninety that afternoon, and he was wearing a navy blue suit. I saw him pull a white handkerchief from his coat pocket and mop sweat from his brow. His swagger was gone and he blinked at the concrete floor. Nerves, I thought, as if he knew Willie Collins was going to be too much for him. Some men were that way — they wanted a wild filly they could break — if they were man enough. I had my doubts about Floyd's manliness. But what did it matter? I was less concerned about the wad in his pants and more about the wad in his pocket.

Floyd's father stood next to him, the notorious bootlegger John Carter. Floyd and I had been out to dinner with his parents—steaks, baked potatoes, and drinking colas out of respect for Prohibition. I don't know if they approved of me. They hardly asked me any questions, and John Carter was distracted by people coming up to him and shaking his hand. He was a big shot pretty much everywhere he went. Now he puffed on a cigar and watched the road, eyeing every vehicle that cruised past the courthouse. By his side Mrs. Carter, a pretty woman on the plump side, wore a silky dress and a stole made of two brown minks that almost looked alive, one wrapped around her neck and biting the behind of the other to hold them in place. It was far too hot for a fur of any kind, but I assumed she was going for effect rather than comfort.

My folks waited for me on the courthouse steps. With her hair pulled back in a neat bun, May had a simple elegance about her. Protective of his only daughter, Pop kept his eye on John Carter, but he should have known by now his only daughter could stand up for herself even next to the likes of the Carter clan. When the court officer called us in, May handed me a small bouquet of asters, stems tied with a pink ribbon. There was no music, no lighted candles, no wedding veil. It was a quick ceremony interrupted twice by an "ahem" from John Carter, a sort of cough. Approval or disapproval, I wasn't sure.

Afterward, Pop slapped Floyd manlike on the back.

"You got your hands full, young man," he said.

"Don't I know it, Jim." Floyd should have shown Pop respect by calling him Mr. Collins, but I supposed we were all family now.

May hugged me. She smelled of rosewater. "You keep following your dreams, Willie," she said.

"Don't you worry about me, Mama," I said. "I'm shooting for the stars."

John Carter edged May aside. Then he stood in front of his new daughter-in-law for a heartbeat before leaning forward and kissing me on the lips. I was not one to be shocked by much, but a kiss from my husband's father, on the lips, no less, was—well, it was unexpected. My own father had never kissed me. I felt Floyd bristle beside me, but he kept his mouth shut.

The top was down on the convertible. As he had never done before, Floyd held open the passenger door for me. This time I didn't ask to drive. When he pulled onto the road, I tossed the clutch of asters over my head and let the wind take them.

•   •   •

I thought being married to Floyd Carter would satisfy the hunger in my gut, a smoldering desire for power I could never grab hold of on Pop's farm. After rolling cigarettes and standing on my feet all day at the five and dime, I had felt choked. That work was not at all like living. I wanted a life full and real, a life Floyd couldn't give me even with a legendary father. His drivers got paid for running a load of liquor on an all-night trip. For them, eluding the law was a game. The only rule was to have a faster car and to drive for reckless fun as much as for the cash. I'd heard some runners would steal a good car for a single delivery and leave it somewhere on the road. For long trips, there were hideout places they could stop to rest—a farm in an isolated area with a big barn. Sometimes women were brought in for a good time—music, drinking, dancing. And there'd be some fighting. Running liquor leveled the classes. The runners had the supply and the rich had the demand. More than money, making deals with aristocrats gave them a sense most had never felt before—respect. And I yearned for that feeling.

Two years being married to Floyd was no picnic, even though I had to admit our house was more beautiful than any place I'd imagined living, two stories and five columns holding up the roof of a wide porch that wrapped around the side. One night things with Floyd came to a head when we had gone out and he had enjoyed a generous portion of his daddy's liquor. I watched from the lawn he had paid someone to mow as he stumbled up the steps to the front door and fumbled with the key.

"Got it," he said finally. He swiveled his head but didn't look at me. The porch light made him look ghastly even in an expensive suit. "You coming, sweetheart?"

He was in good spirits, at least, and I followed him into the foyer.

"How about a nightcap?" Already he was pulling a bottle of clear liquid from the cabinet. I wished he'd lock it when we went out. In his business, one could never tell when a federal agent would make a raid. But agents knew the consequences of raiding the private domicile of anyone in the Carter family. The punishments were severe and always painful. Sometimes they were deadly.

Rumors flew about those consequences. I didn't know whether Floyd was involved, but sometimes his father would call for him to help with something or other and he'd be out until daybreak. The next day he would be withdrawn and if I asked him what the matter was, he barked it was none of my business. It was better to plead ignorance.

"I'm going to bed," I said that night. "Been a long evening."

He carried a crystal tumbler in his right hand and left hand on the banister, he pulled himself up the stairs behind me. In the bedroom, I hoped he wouldn't spill his drink on the carpet we'd paid a small fortune for.

I unbuttoned my dress and let it drop to the floor, then picked it up and laid it over a chair. At the vanity mirror, I sat in my slip and stroked my hair with a silver-handled brush. Floyd came with accessories I once thought I'd never be able to afford, but for the life of me I couldn't generate affection for him — or even gratitude.

In the mirror's reflection, I watched him set his glass on the nightstand. At least he was careful not to spill and leave a ring on the dark wood. Shrugging out of his jacket, he dropped it onto the bed then pulled the tie out of his shirt collar and tossed it atop the jacket, a routine I resented. There was a closet and wooden hangers, but Floyd Carter was above the menial task of hanging up his clothes. I would have to do it or else crawl in under them.

"You have a good time tonight?" He plopped onto the bed, onto the chenille spread, and reached for his glass.

I sighed. "I guess."

"Didn't you like your chops?"

I pushed my hair into waves.

"All we do is go to speakeasies and parties, drink, and talk about nothing."

"What's wrong with that?" His tone was playful. "If it hadn't been for me dragging you out from behind a cigar counter, you'd be back on your father's farm driving that old steam tractor. You owe me some appreciation."

Floyd the superhero. A regular Zorro, rescuer of the downtrodden. Rescuing me for a life of dullness and monotony. What had made me think money generated happiness?

"Floyd, I'm not ungrateful — I'm bored."

"Ha," he puffed. "You won't have time to get bored when we've got couple of little ones running around and pulling on your apron strings."

Babies weren't part of the plan. Babies would tie me down. I was only twenty, and I had miles of road to travel yet.

"I don't wear aprons," I said. "There's got to be more for a woman than looking nice and having babies."

Floyd sipped his drink and raised his eyebrows. "What do you want to do, Willie, run for President?"

I turned on the silk-upholstered bench to look at him.

"You don't get it, do you? Your daddy's got so much money you never had a chance to want something so bad it nearly strangled you."

"My daddy works hard for his money." His jovial mood had turned. We'd been on this stage before, but I knew my lines by heart.

"Selling bootleg liquor?"

He jerked his chin toward my feet. "I don't hear you complaining about those Italian leather shoes you're wearing."

I pitched the brush onto the vanity top and tried to control my anger. "I'm tired. Let's just go to bed."

Floyd got up and came behind me, bent to kiss my neck. "I can make us some adventure."

"Floyd, you're about as exciting as a boll weevil." I had done everything to avoid having sex with Floyd. I'd even seen a doctor to make sure I wouldn't end up with an idiot child like its father.

He stood up and looked at himself in the mirror above my face.

"Suit yourself. Anyway, I've got to meet with Daddy in the morning. Sheriff Bridges put his best driver in the slammer." He started unbuttoning his shirt. "He and the commonwealth's attorney are wearing gold cufflinks and gold fillings in their teeth paid for with the money Daddy's handed over to leave his drivers alone. There's nothing worse than lawmen so crooked even a crooked businessman can't trust them."

Now I was interested. I leaned forward and wiped lipstick from my mouth with a tissue.

"I could drive for him."

"You? I don't want my wife going to work. Especially not that work." His expression had changed. I could deal with him angry but when I mentioned his father, his face showed dread.

"You leave that between me and your father. I'll go with you to see him tomorrow."

"I don't like it, Willie."

I got up and stepped out of my expensive shoes. Now I had to look up at him, a bantam hen confronting the rooster.

"Floyd Carter, I don't give a hot damn what you like."

•   •   •

That morning, wanting to make an impression, I wore a good dress and had steamed my hair into curls. At his Rocky Mount office, John Carter sat behind a polished wood desk. The aroma of fresh coffee drifted from a china cup in front of him, the cup atop a delicate-looking saucer. Until that moment I hadn't realized what a handsome man he was, even for middle age.

Two wingback chairs faced the desk, and Floyd claimed one of them. I stayed standing. Carter looked up and frowned at his son as if annoyed by his visit.

"Morning, Daddy," Floyd said.

Carter ignored him and set his attention on me.

"Willie — good to see you." His voice was stern but pleasant. He turned to Floyd. "Don't you have some business to tend to?"

Floyd looked confused. "You wanted to see me about — "

"It can wait." He didn't take his eyes off me. "Have a seat, Willie."

I caught the flush on Floyd's cheeks. His father was in command, Floyd not even the appointed heir apparent.

"I'll see you at lunch, Willie," he said.

When Floyd was out of the room, I took the reins.

"Mr. Carter, I — "

"I prefer you call me John," he interrupted.

"Yes, sir — John."

"Coffee?" He pointed four fingers at his cup. I had gotten used to drinking from china, but I shook my head, wanting all my attention on the conversation.

"How are things with my son?" Carter asked.

I hesitated, not sure what the man wanted to hear.

"All right."

Carter picked up the cue. "Anything wrong?"

"Naw. I'm just not used to being a wife."

"Your mother got used to it, didn't she?" He offered me a soft smile and I was touched that he mentioned May. Little did he know May might have gotten used to it, but she would never enjoy that life—except for Pop. After twenty-two years together, I was sure they still adored each other. I would never feel that way with Floyd.

"My mother was different. More like a partner on the farm."

Carter sipped from his cup, eyeing me over the rim. Slowly he placed the cup back on its saucer and leaned back in his big desk chair.

"How'd you like to partner with me?"

I could hardly breathe. Working with John Carter was exactly what I wanted, but I didn't expect him to suggest it first. If the wingback chair had been a seat in a rail car, the train was barreling full speed ahead. But I had to play it coy. I had to be patient, bat the ball back to him.

"What do you mean?"

"I hear you can drive pretty good."

There it was—the first outline of a dream taking shape.

"I'd say that's about right. I learned out of necessity."

Carter got up, came around the desk, and perched on the arm of the other wing chair. His knees almost touched my arm.

"Floyd got you a Stutz, as I understand."

"He did, yes." I loved that automobile. A Stutz Bearcat, low and fast, a yellow flash when I wound it out.

"It giving you any trouble?"

I wouldn't have called it trouble, not the way I handled it.

"It's a little light. I have to watch it around the curves."

Carter considered for a second. "Think you can handle something heavier?"

I felt a naughty grin crack my face. "I like something heavy under me."

Carter looked pleased and allowed himself three subtle nods. I knew we understood each other.

"I've got some fast cars," he said. "And all you'd have to do is go like a bat out of hell and stop where I tell you to stop. It'll be night work. You can snooze all day if you want."

"Drive a car? That's all I have to do?" Driving was reward enough, but I suspected more was coming. And I wanted more.

"You'll settle up with me," Carter said. "You'll get fifty dollars a trip, half of which comes to me."

My confidence expanded. He wanted a driver, and I could drive, all right.

"Why do I have to split it with you if I'm doing the driving?"

"Because, Willie —" He leaned forward and laid his hand on my knee. "I'm the boss."

9.
Jimmy — 1924

You haven't lived until you've spent time in the Blue Ridge. The soft air filtered through pine boughs is better than the best whiskey. Mountain streams like veins carry pure water as gifts to the creatures below. Winters when the sun rises behind Bent Mountain, its peak is frosted with cold powdered sugar. Early mornings, working men climb into their overalls or their mufti and go out to make deliveries, operate machinery, slaughter, or milk. A horse whinnies and a cow in her low, mournful voice calls the farmer to relieve her udders. Afterward, the scratch of a match head catching fire, lighting a burner or a cigarette or both, mingles with the aromas of coffee, shaving cream, musk, and sweat. Sizzling sausage, clinking pottery, the ting of spoon stirring cream into coffee — cream from a farmer's own cows or his neighbors' — is morning's music.

At night, fireflies flicker in the fields, looking for meals and mates. The stars are so close you can reach up and touch them, and meteors paint streaks of light across the black curtain of sky. On moonless nights you can't see your hand in front of your face, but country people know the roads and trails so well we can navigate them in our sleep.

It was on such nights that I courted Dottie. We were both almost out of our teens, and she allowed me to touch her in places I'd never touched before — except with Lila. Lila had taught me how to pleasure a woman, and I did my best to show Dottie what I had learned. One night we were lying on a blanket in her daddy's field so we could watch the stars. Some said there were aliens in these parts living in caves and once in a while they got into their sky ships and went looking for whatever their people needed. Food, excitement, or maybe love.

I brought a jar of Pop's hard cider which we took turns sipping, and we were both in a frisky mood. Suddenly a streak crossed the sky—a shooting star leaving a long, thin wake of sparks.

"It's a sign," Dottie breathed. I had my hand up her skirt and hoped she meant it was a good omen. I tested my luck, and she opened for me. Those aliens were fortunate, indeed.

It must've been sweet for Willie to drive on those nights, windows down letting in the scents of alfalfa, sweet corn, melons decaying in a harvested field. Those smells couldn't be overpowered even by the exhaust of a multi-valve engine operating at high revolutions per minute. More valves cool the cylinder head, which Willie would need at high speeds. She tutored me in how to get more power out of a motor, and I swear she sounded like she knew what she was talking about.

While most women were getting mail-order catalogs from Montgomery Ward and Sears, running their fingers over pictures of new hats, silk stockings, and flowered dresses, Willie had her sleeves rolled to her elbows and grease dripping from her fingers. She had a determination I'd never seen in another woman—not May, and certainly not Dottie. But Dottie had other qualities that charmed me.

10.
Willie

Near midnight I drove the Stutz to Burnt Chimney, fifteen miles south of Roanoke, and parked beside the Blackwater Filling Station where it would be out of sight. It was a clear, cool night with no wind, the kind of night you might hear a train whistle in the distance or a dog howling at an invisible intruder. A night of new beginnings, as if the switch operator pulled the lever to change the track, sending the locomotive in a different direction. I felt a quiver of excitement on such a night.

"You made it, Willie," John Carter said. He smiled—straight teeth, strong jaw—and touched the brim of his hat in a salute.

"Evening, John," I said. "You think I'd miss the action?"

"Never crossed my mind," he said. He put an arm around me and hugged me to him as if we were pals—or as if he owned me.

Under Blackwater's streetlamp, a thin man dressed in coveralls with the Blackwater logo came toward us from the station with a gallon jug in each hand.

"Give those to Charlie, Joe," Carter told him.

"Those some of your associates?" I asked.

Carter nodded toward Joe. "That's J. O. Shively," he said. "He owns the station. Keeps some of our stock in a room under lock and key."

Joe approached a fellow in pleated trousers, shirt cuffs pushed up his forearms.

"The other's Charlie Sharpe, one of our best drivers."

Charlie looked to be around twenty. A curl of his caramel-color hair fell onto his forehead, and even under the filling station streetlamp I could tell his eyes were cornflower blue. Something moved in my chest, an odd feeling I had trouble identifying. Probably my imagination. I looked away but when my eyes drew back to Charlie, there was the feeling again.

Joe handed the jugs to Charlie who loaded them into a compartment of a black Ford.

"That'll do it, Joe," I heard Charlie say.

"You coming in for another run tonight?" Joe asked.

"Depends on what Stuart's up to. If the roads are open, you'll see me in a few hours." Charlie's voice had a soft southern lilt. I sensed kindness in him. A kind bootlegger? Who was this man?

"I've got a cot in the back room if you need it later," Joe said. "You know the knock."

"Sure, Joe. Thanks," Charlie said.

I followed Carter to the car where Charlie adjusted the jugs. The Ford had a square body with bug-eye headlights like any other Model A on the road. I could see a compartment under the seat crammed with glass containers of moonshine.

"This'll be a short run to Roanoke, Willie," Carter said. "You know the route?"

"Any fool knows how to get to Roanoke," I said.

"You're not going any fool's route. You'll have to divert onto some mountain roads."

"I know those roads. Been driving them most my life."

Carter sniggered. "Well, that's a hell of a long time."

"Long enough to know I can handle this rattletrap." I didn't like my driving skills called into question, but I wanted to convince Carter I was up to the job.

"Let's hope so," he said. Carter turned to Charlie. "You all set?"

"Couldn't get another drop of liquor in this rig with an eyedropper." Charlie looked at me. "Who's this fella?"

I had dressed in trousers, a button-up shirt and a brimmed hat, thinking if I was going to drive like a man, I ought to look like one. Seeing Charlie Sharpe, I wished I had reconsidered.

"This fella is my daughter-in-law Willie. She'll be driving tonight. I want you to go with her, show her some tricks."

When Charlie scanned me from my oxfords to my fedora, I felt my arms go numb and balled my hands into fists to bring sensation back.

"I've seen you around," Charlie said.

I wanted to ask where. I hoped he hadn't seen me with Floyd. On the other hand, it wouldn't be a bad thing to be noticed with the kingpin's son. I wanted Charlie to know I had some status in this business.

He patted the Ford's hood. "This is the buggy I usually drive. You'll have to be careful on the turns. The weight can capsize you."

"Do I look like a turtle to you?" I said.

Charlie tipped his hat. "No, ma'am, you sure don't look like no turtle. But you'd better let me tell you about this automobile. She looks like a Ford." He lifted the hood. "But there's a Cadillac engine under here with three two-barrel carburetors and fifteen forward gears."

"Fifteen—?"

"You heard right. Loaded, you've got over a thousand pounds of cargo, so you'll need the power."

I hadn't driven anything with more than three forward gears. And I didn't have much time tonight to figure out what to do with the other twelve.

Charlie shut the hood and pointed to the rear tires. "Those flaps are made of steel in case the federal agents try to shoot out your tires."

"Shoot out my—?" I felt like I couldn't get out a complete sentence.

"But I don't expect you'll have any trouble tonight."

When headlights flashed across the side of the Ford, Carter looked toward the approaching car. "Looks like trouble got a head start on you," he said.

A short man with a hefty build got out of the car. He wore an expensive-looking suit tailored to hide his bulk. His stern look gave him the appearance of someone who likes to control people around him.

Carter put his face close to mine.

"That's Ewell Stuart," he said, "Roanoke's commonwealth attorney who prosecutes misdemeanor and felony cases. He's descended from Civil War general Jeb Stuart and won't let anyone forget it." Carter spat onto the pavement.

"You going to cancel the run?" I asked.

"No—I'll take care of him."

Stuart sauntered toward the loaded Ford.

"Seems to me it's pretty late to be going for a drive in the country."

"Never too late for an evening under the stars," Carter said.

Stuart lifted his face to the sky where clouds were gathering.

"Looking like there might be rain." He leveled his eyes at Carter. "And anyway, you won't be seeing any stars through the ceiling of a jail cell."

"Now look, Stuart," Carter said, "the county's jails are already overcrowded. You're sending people to the prison in Salem so they're not sleeping on top of each other here."

"And I'd hate to think of a man as stylish as yourself wasting away behind bars, Carter. Salem or otherwise." Stuart tossed his hand toward the trunk of the Ford. "You want to show me what you're hauling in this vehicle?"

Carter hesitated. "Tell you what—I'll show you something better inside." He patted Stuart on the shoulder and turned him toward the station building. I watched him pull some bills from his pocket and count out several as they walked.

"Listen, Willie," Charlie said, "you don't see anything, you don't say anything and you'll be clear to go."

So that was the way things worked.

"All right, then," I said. "Let's get this show on the road."

I slid in behind the wheel, and Charlie climbed aboard the passenger seat. He pointed to the gearshift rod.

"Think about a three-story building," he said. "On each level, you've got five gears. The first floor is deep low gear with the most torque." When he reached over, his knuckles grazed my thigh. He put his hand over mine on the gearshift stick and I shivered. Even in night's chill his hand was warm and I felt heat rise to my cheeks.

"Flip this switch on the shift level to get to the second floor." His finger guided mine to the switch. "That's low range. When you get up a head of steam, flip the switch again to take you to the third floor for top speed."

I had to pay attention, had to focus. Shifting was no problem, but I'd have to listen to the engine to sense when to press the switch.

"You may not need to top out tonight," he said, withdrawing his hand.

"You want to show me again?" I said, wishing for another touch of his hand.

"I think you've got it," he said. "If we get on a straightaway, wind her out and see what she can do."

I admit I was a bit flustered—switches, gears, and Charlie so close.

"Thanks, Mr.—"

"It's Charlie," he said. "Charlie Sharpe."

It took a second to remember to breathe.

"Thanks, Charlie Sharpe."

"Okay, then," he said. "You ready to roll?"

I shifted into gear and the wheels squealed on the pavement as the Ford exited the filling station. The car was a cheetah with the strength of a bush elephant. Driving a rig like this Ford was going to take some getting used to.

"You're a natural," Charlie said.

I would not disappoint him.

Ahead less than a mile, I spied a roadblock. As I drew closer, it looked like the sawhorse barrier had been pulled aside. When the Ford passed, Charlie saluted the attending police officer.

"Well, I declare," I said. "You've got some magic mischief in you, Charlie Sharpe."

"Take the next right," he said, all business now. "It's a dirt road, so pay attention. There'll be a curve and then a straightaway. I want you to open her up."

I made the turn, careful about the automobile's weight.

"All right, then," I said. "Let's see what this baby can do."

On the straightaway, the engine growled and the Ford tossed up dust behind the wheels. By the second floor we were doing eighty. I shifted through the gears and smiled over at Charlie.

"You ready?" I said.

He ran his tongue over his bottom lip, wetting it. "Ready."

By the third floor we were up over a hundred. A hundred-ten with a full cargo of clear liquid worth hundreds of dollars.

"I believe you've passed the test," Charlie said. "Better save the power for when you really need it." His voice didn't quaver. He wasn't afraid, and he had earned my respect. I had a feeling I was going to get know this fellow Charlie Sharpe better.

11.
Jimmy — 1925

It had to happen eventually — I mean Willie meeting her match. I reckoned it'd take a strong type to tame my sister. Growing up, I thought of Willie more as a brother. She was built solid, preferred pants to dresses, liked a drink of Pop's shine when he'd let her, and would spit in your eye if you called her a lady. What I didn't factor was Willie turning soft as a dewy calf around a fella who treats her kindly. Charlie Sharpe was that sort.

I guessed I had met my match, too. When Dottie told me she was in the family way, there was nothing to do but take her down to city hall and sign the marriage license. I had no regrets. Dottie and I were meant for each other, as if the planets and all the angels had willed it. Being a father was going to take some getting used to, but I had most of a year to think and plan. Things were going to work out for us. Probably better than they worked out for Willie.

12.
Willie—1925

Summer evenings in the Blue Ridge are magic, stars bright against a black sky, air fresh with a trace of manure. On such a night, Blackwater Filling Station was quiet except for the soft clink of glass jars I loaded into the car. Charlie had coached me for three runs, and after weeks of driving solo, I knew the routine. Pack the jars tight under the seat, press cloth between to keep them from rattling, and cover the whole cargo with burlap. Then drive like I'm possessed.

When a cop car pulled into the lot, I straightened up. A man in a brown uniform struggled to get out from behind the wheel. Deputy Sheriff Lewis Bridges had been around the filling station before. He was known to pick up a jug of moonshine from time to time as payment for clearing the road when a delivery came through.

The deputy waddled toward me. I believed he enjoyed more than healthy portions of his wife's fried chicken.

"You on duty tonight, Sheriff?" I said.

"You don't see any sheriff's badge do you?" His double chin muffled his voice.

"No, sir, I don't." Best to be polite. Badge or no badge, Bridges worked for the county.

"You mind your business and nobody'll get into trouble. You got that?"

"Right, sir." I closed the trunk and watched the porpoise swim toward the station building.

After a minute, John Carter came from the station and approached where I stood waiting for instructions.

"I want you to take this load to Baltimore," he said. "Bridges has opened the barricades, but keep your eyes peeled. If you're not back by breakfast, I'll send someone after you."

I stuck my right leg under the steering wheel, getting ready to mount my fast horse.

"I like my eggs over easy," I said. "Keep the yolks runny. And sausage on the side."

· · ·

The next afternoon, I had my head under the hood of the Stutz when Floyd came from the house.

"What're you doing, Willie?" he asked.

I didn't look up. "Adding a little zing to this rattletrap. See—" With a greasy finger I pointed to a mechanism in the engine. "This air compressor gives the intake cycle more oxygen. That burns more fuel, which adds power. I should be able to get this rig up to one-twenty easy."

"All you think about is cars," Floyd said. "You been out all night five times in the last week. And the week before that, too."

"That is correct." I raised my head and glared at him. "And?"

"People are talking. I don't like being talked about."

"I'm real sorry about that, Floyd, but driving is the only time I feel alive."

"There's no sense to it. I've got plenty of money."

Floyd always rankled me. He was incapable of having a respectful conversation. Everything was a challenge, an argument.

"You mean your daddy's got money. Unlike you, I'm earning mine."

"You've got everything you want—a closet full of nice dresses, fur coats, diamonds. Why can't you be happy for once?"

"There are things you don't comprehend about women," I said. If truth be known, I didn't think there was much he did comprehend.

"Oh, I comprehend women." He pointed a finger in my face. "It's you I don't understand." He grabbed my arm and shoved me away from the car. "Go inside and wash yourself. You're covered in filth."

I came at him with my fists. When he grabbed my forearms, his strength surprised me, but I broke loose, jerked my hand away and slapped him hard across the cheek.

"Don't..you..ever..tell me what to do," I said.

Floyd dropped his hands. "I've had about enough of this."

I planted my fists on my hips. "So have I. I've had so much I'm choking on it." I picked up a wrench and stuck my head under the car's hood. In an attempt to dismiss him, I added, "We're done, Floyd."

"Now, wait a minute, Willie," he said, his voice not quite apologetic but leaning that way.

I pulled my head up, tossed the wrench onto the lawn, and let the hood drop shut. Ignoring Floyd, I swirled the crank to start the engine. When I was pleased with its growl, I got in and shifted into gear. Then I peeled out, leaving Floyd standing by the curb with a helpless look on his mug.

•   •   •

I hadn't seen Charlie Sharpe at Blackwater for a few weeks, but tonight there he was, piling whiskey jugs into a pickup truck. My mood had been dark since the falling out with Floyd.

Failure hadn't been part of the plan, but I knew the marriage was doomed from the start. Even so, I felt my seams fraying. Floyd had given me entry to a good life with expensive frills, but silks and pricey shoes weren't enough. Neither was the diamond I had the dentist set in my front tooth. Those indulgences earned me the respect of men and the admiration of women, but because of my line of work and the people I worked with, no one dared get close to Willie Carter. My reputation for driving and the threat of consequences if anyone rubbed my father-in-law the wrong way made me feel isolated and, to be honest, lonely. I had no close friends—even Lois and the other women I'd worked with kept their distance. Only driving gave me a thrill and when I was on the road, my spirits floated on the Appalachian air. They especially floated seeing Charlie.

"Evening, Willie," he said. His boyish grin got me every time.

I nodded at him. "Charlie" was all I said before my voice failed me.

"I hear you quit working for John Carter." Charlie didn't waste time. Time in the bootleg world was money.

"I guess word travels fast." My hand found the back of my neck, and I studied my shadow cast by the station's light. "Quit the whole Carter clan, in fact. The divorce'll be final next month." I wanted him to know I was not tied to Floyd anymore and was disappointed when he didn't congratulate me. "I hear you got out, too." I didn't know the details but figured John Carter was holding off on full payment for a night's delivery. Charlie could do better running his own business.

"That's right." He waited for me to raise my eyes to his. "How'd you like to drive for me?"

"I was hoping you'd ask." In truth, when Carter told me he couldn't keep me on if I was no longer part of the family, I wondered whether any new doors would open. In small towns, reputations loomed large. Everyone knew everyone in the business, and everyone in the business knew Willie Carter could drive fast cars.

"There's just one thing —" Charlie said.

"I'm willing to entertain one thing," I said. Hell, I'd probably entertain several things. I wasn't desperate — at least, not yet. I'd taken a room in a boarding house, but the last thing I wanted was to travel a bumpy highway in reverse.

"You won't be carrying. You'll be driving pilot — no liquor."

"What's the point?" Drivers knew the roads. They didn't need a pilot and, anyway, no driver could keep up with me if I was free of the cargo weight.

"The point is, the feds are clamping down. Bridges would as soon lock you away if they think it'll make it look like they aren't patronizing the —" Charlie looked toward the station where the liquor was stashed. "The product of the industry."

"So we're on our own, I guess?" I liked the word "we." Charlie and me — in business together.

"We've got to outsmart them," he said. "You drive and the feds won't know you're empty. You'll be the decoy."

"If they don't know I'm empty, won't they come after me anyway?"

"I've bolted steel plates to the car's body in case they try to slow you down."

"You mean shoot at me." I hadn't figured on being a target for gunfire. I could drive fast, but could I outrun a bullet?

"If a slug comes at you, two forces start acting on it immediately — gravity and air resistance, both slowing it down," Charlie said. "If you're far enough ahead, it will drop and might hit the metal guards over the wheels." He patted the roof of the Ford. "This ride's got plenty of horses under the hood, so either outrun them or outmaneuver them."

I searched his eyes. "You want me to take the law on a wild ride and clear the road for the real haul." It wasn't a question. I was telling him I understood.

He blinked. "You're good at fancy driving, aren't you?"

What other options did I have? "I guess we'll see, won't we?"

Charlie offered a bewitching smile. "Let's test it out tonight. I'll take the truck and you'll be in the Ford. Head toward Washington. We've got a couple deliveries in the city."

Washington was six hours north. He could get there in four, especially if I could get him through without a hitch.

"Ready when you are," I said.

"I'll be a mile behind you, but don't look back."

May had told me the myth of Orpheus, the musician who went to Hades to retrieve his dead lover. The sap couldn't resist turning around to be sure she was behind him. If she had gone ahead of him, they'd both have made it out of hell. I wouldn't have to look. I had a sixth sense when it came to driving and a seventh sense when it came to Charlie Sharpe.

•   •   •

The Ford was doing ninety when I barreled through the sawhorses Bridges had set up. The coppers would have to board their ponies, so I held steady to give them time to build up speed. Even without carrying, they could nail me for wild driving—if they could catch me. But catching Willie Carter would take some clever driving and a heap of luck.

I was past Lexington, almost to Staunton and feeling fine when the nearly impossible happened, the eerie sheen of headlights over my shoulder. The sheriff must have called the law farther north to join the party. The road was almost dead flat, and I shifted into the upper floor, letting the horses have their head. The speedometer needle neared ninety-five. I could do better and inched toward the century mark, covering thirty miles in minutes.

When I jerked my head to the right, in my margin of sight I caught a shadow leaning out the passenger window, an arm attached to the shadow. And the hand at the end of the arm could damn well have a finger on the trigger of a revolver. If they couldn't catch me, their lead might.

I heard the ping of the bullet on a wheel shield and said a silent thanks to Charlie. But the game wasn't over. A second bullet screamed over the Ford's roof. Then I heard a ping at the back window. A hot pellet cut the air beside my elbow and buried itself in the dashboard.

Anger rippled through me, but I couldn't lose focus.

"Okay, you chumps," I breathed.

Two hundred yards up the road, a shortcut to Charlottesville required a sharp right turn. At best, my pursuers would have to slow down on the curve. Right before the turn, I slammed the brakes and twisted the wheel. The unloaded car easily skidded into the opposite direction and headed straight for the oncoming headlights. I heard the cruiser's brakes screech as the tires made a futile attempt to grab the pavement. Swerving past the driver's side, I saw the coppers' vehicle careen around the curve on two wheels.

I parked the Ford onto a treed access path leading to the Blue Ridge Rail Tunnel and turned off the lights. Blowing a deep breath, I stretched out my arms. My elbow felt sore, and I pressed my palm against it. The cloth was damp, and in the starlight I saw a dark sticky substance on my hand. Blood. Not much blood—not enough to fill a thimble. And no pain. I must have hit the arm against something. Nothing to worry about.

I laughed—a loud horselaugh—and flashed to an image of Pop sitting by the stove reading the newspaper, glasses sliding down his nose, nodding off, May in the rocker next to him knitting or hooking a rug. That would never be my life—

couldn't possibly be. My brain was hard-wired for speed, for the thrill of the chase. For danger and risk. For exhilaration. But it was more than that. Driving fast required concentration that blanked out everything else—Floyd, hoeing potatoes on Pop's farm, routine and boredom. When I drove, every nerve in my body was alert, every sense engaged. Nothing mattered but the wheel, the gearshift, and the road ahead. I was untouchable when I drove. I was divine.

Within a few minutes the cruiser roared past in the opposite direction, this time with its siren blaring. A pickup truck pulled to the side to let them by, a truck no lawman expected to be carrying contraband. I had done as Charlie asked. I had cleared the road and nearly taken a pellet for him. He had better show me his appreciation.

•   •   •

At Blackwater, I steered the Ford into the garage and closed it up. I napped in the Stutz until nearly dawn when Charlie returned in the pickup. Then I climbed in beside him.

"We had a good run tonight." He took a roll of bills from his pocket, peeled off four twenties, and handed them to me.

"The boys up north are generous," I said.

He put an arm around my shoulders. "I told them a pretty woman was escorting the goods."

"It's nice doing business with you, Charlie Sharpe," I said.

He pulled me closer. "My pleasure, ma'am." When he kissed me, I curled an arm over his chest and kissed him back.

"Let's go," he mumbled into my hair.

"Where to? It's nearly daylight."

"I've got to get some food into you. You haven't lived until you've tasted my fried eggs and scrapple."

•   •   •

Charlie got the iron skillet from a hook in his bungalow kitchen and broke some eggs into a bowl. The place was simple—two easy chairs, a table against the wall with a bench. No Chippendale chairs like I'd grown used to. But I liked the masculine feel, the smoky, woodsy aroma, the cool breeze tickling the muslin curtains.

"You have a bathtub in this joint?" I asked. "I'd like to wash off some road dust."

"Sure," he said. "Need any help?"

"Think I can handle a knob and spigot."

Charlie laughed. "Breakfast will be ready when you are."

While the tub filled, I peeled out of my work clothes. The clawfoot tub was wide and deep, and I eased into the steaming water and stretched out. Within a few minutes, a soft knock came on the door, and Charlie entered with a clean bath towel.

"Thought you'd need this." His chest was bare, and he had another towel tucked around his waist. Unlike Floyd whose chest was a forest of curly black fur, Charlie's was as smooth as a teenager's.

"I'll be out in a minute," I said.

"Don't bother. Plenty of room for two." Dropping his towel, he stepped in behind me, his legs straddling me. I could feel his warmth, the muscles of his thighs.

"Hand me the soap." He rubbed his hands on the Ivory until I heard the squish of suds. Then his hands were slipping over my skin, his thumbs pressing into the tight places, loosening and relaxing me. I wanted to ask what magic he wove. Instead, I sighed as he dribbled rinse water over my skin. When he slipped his arms around me, he touched my elbow and I shuddered. The arm had stopped bleeding, but now it was stinging.

"What is it?" he said.

"It's nothing." I corrected myself. "Hardly anything."

"That's a fresh wound. They shot at you, didn't they?"

When I didn't answer, he said, "Let me fix you up. I've got bandages."

"It'll wait." I leaned against his chest and he soaped my legs, cupped my breasts. When he reached between my legs, I gasped and pressed myself into his hands. The water had cooled, but heat poured through me like slow moving lava. Heaviness overcame me, and I melted into him.

"You better be careful," I panted. "I could get used to this."

He mumbled into my hair, "Wouldn't want breakfast to get cold, and I've got to see about that arm."

"Not yet," I said. "Not quite yet."

I felt my heart thrusting blood through my arteries, through my breasts, waking the nipples, my whole body on alert. Where his fingers pressed into me, slippery with soap, an electric cord sent sparks over my skin. Bolts of lightning shot into my brain and I gasped and turned my face to his, opening my mouth to his, finding his tongue with my tongue.

When I found my breath, I whispered, "Lord have mercy."

"First time?" Charlie asked.

I could manage only a slow nod. Charlie smiled, his pearly teeth glinting under the bathroom light. If a man feels no greater pleasure than pleasuring a woman, then Charlie must have been well pleased. I was his woman now.

Slowly he lifted himself from the water and snagged the towel he had dropped. "Breakfast," he said. "And a bandage for that elbow."

I was surprised to discover my legs were weak, and he helped me from the tub.

"Lift your arms." With the fresh towel he dried my back. "Spread your legs," he said, and I obeyed. If he had asked me to walk across live embers, I would have.

Gently he wiped the inside of my thighs, the tender spot he had explored.

"Where are my clothes?" I said.

"I've got a robe you can put on." Plaid flannel hung on a hook behind the bathroom door, and he wrapped the robe around me, the soft cotton smelling of aftershave and wild mint. Then he opened the medicine cabinet behind the mirror and pushed bottles around until he found bandage material. I winced again as he doctored the wound. No man, especially not Floyd, had done for me in this way. But Charlie Sharpe was not any man. I knew with all my knowing Charlie Sharpe was someone special.

He put on a sweatshirt and loose pants and poured us each a healthy shot of liquor. We drank slowly and ate quickly. Then he lit a cigarette and leaned back in his chair.

"We've got to get some rest now," he said.

"You asking me to stay here?"

"Bed's big enough for two." But rest was not what either of us had in mind.

A small lamp glowed next to the bed, but I didn't bother turning it off. I wanted to see this man, to study his marble body. Letting the robe fall to the floor, I slipped under the cover and watched him take his time lifting his shirt over his head. His chest rippled when he tossed the shirt toward a wooden chair. I met his eyes but when he dropped his trousers, my gaze fell to his manhood greeting me in joyful fullness. Wet seeped from me, slicking my thighs, and a longing gripped me. I'd never desired a man as much as I desired this one.

He crawled on top of me, hands beside my head bracing himself, trapping me like a rabbit caught between a wolf's paws. His scent was smoke and scrapple and soap, and a masculine, musky scent, too, that brought me to an almost unbearable craving for him. I wanted him to devour me and wiggled myself lower in the bed, inviting him in. He offered me an evil grin and worked his way down my body, kissing first my neck, then pausing at each nipple, flicking his tongue over them. A moan escaped me—a tortured moan I didn't recognize as my own voice.

When he reached my belly, I shivered. Pulling the cover over his head, he felt his way in the darkness to my most private place where no man's face, no man's tongue had ever been. He lapped at me like a cat at a bowl of cream, circling my magic button. He was insistent, relentless, and I gripped the cover as if it would keep me from catching fire. But fire shot through me and the soles of my feet sparked. And as I cried out, he was there, suddenly, inside me, slipping in and out of me. I tightened myself to keep him deep, but each time he pulled away, I was brought nearly to tears until he found me again. Then I laughed and laughed again as I felt him pulsing, trembling, filling me. A slow groan escaped him and he buried his forehead in the crook where my neck met my shoulder. I wove my fingers into the strands of his hair and felt that same enchantment that had drawn me to him at the filling station—an electricity that brought me more alive than even the high speed of night driving.

With a heavy arm, he reached for the lamp and turned off the light.

•　　•　　•

Charlie had drawn a thin curtain against the light, but I woke to soft afternoon sun slanting through the cloth. His bedroom wasn't as grand as Floyd Carter's, and our clothes—both our clothes—were strewn over chairs. I didn't care.

I turned my face to Charlie's and we made love again. Daylight lovemaking is quicker, less desperate, more alert. In daylight there's an understanding that you are in familiar territory—a bond has formed sweet with mutual approval.

Afterward, Charlie lit a cigarette.

"I've got eight suppliers and plenty of demand," he said, blowing smoke at the ceiling. "If you're up for it, we'll be working close together most nights."

"I wouldn't call this work." He handed me his cigarette, from his lips to mine, and I took a puff.

He looked at me, his eyes tender. "No sense in you living in a boarding house when I've got plenty of room here."

"You asking me to move in?" My voice was husky. If this was a dream, I didn't ever want to wake up.

"It would make things easier."

"I like easy."

Charlie kissed my bare shoulder.

"Willie Carter Sharpe," I said. "It has a nice ring."

He broke into a lazy grin. "Baby, you keep driving like you do, and I don't care what you call yourself."

13.
Jimmy — 1927

Dottie and I had taken a small apartment in Roanoke, and I paid the rent by working at the sawmill up in Fincastle County and doing carpentry on the side. We named our little boy George. He was a handful, but Dottie managed housekeeping and caring for George, and she took in ironing whenever we ran short. When May learned we had a second child on the way, she said it looked like I was going to make something of myself. She meant something besides farming and being called country. May hated that word. To her country meant you were a rustic, you were common. To me being country was a state of mind. We looked out for our neighbors and cared for our family through good times and bad. Country people didn't let their heads get too big.

Willie was doing everything she could not to seem country — wearing nice clothes and holding her head high. May liked that her daughter was living the high life. But May didn't know the whole story. I mean the illegal part. Or how Willie got involved with Charlie Sharpe. When a gal fancies a fellow as much as Willie fancied Charlie, they can't help how things move right along.

But whenever I saw my sister I got a sense something was missing. Her life had taken a different path than mine, both of us working on opposite sides of the law. I had a wife and a growing family. Eventually I acquired man's best friend. Truth is, the dog loved Willie more than it loved me maybe because she's the one who rescued it. Or maybe the dog rescued Willie. I'll let her tell you about it.

14.
Willie—1927

I moved my things into Charlie's place and was piloting for him two or three trips a night. Money flowed into our hands, and I fixed up the bungalow. Waxed the wood floors, bought new draperies, new furniture. I paid the moving men to take the old stuff to the dump. Not that the old pieces were worn out, but I wanted to put my own stamp on our place.

We were too recognizable to go out much, but some afternoons when I forced myself to leave Charlie's bed, I buttoned into a nice dress, buckled on soft leather shoes, and pulled a hat down over my eyes to hide my face. A girl with money had to shop, after all. I frequented the best Roanoke establishments where discreet salesgirls elbowed each other out of the way to wait on me. The gals made thirty cents an hour, and they knew I was good for a tip, especially on a hundred-dollar sale. Camelhair and tweeds for winter, linen and twill for summer. Afterward, I carried the bags to the millinery shop for a custom-made hat to match the coat or dress, fanning tens and twenties from my purse for the purchases. Finally, to Davidsons to pick out a shirt for Charlie and a silk tie for which he planted kisses on my forehead and cheeks.

Some nights when I drove three hundred miles piloting, I sang songs to myself to help me stay awake and on the mettle.

"Puttin' on the Ritz" made my foot heavy on the gas pedal, and I imagined myself dripping in diamonds and fur singing in front of a posh audience in the Plaza Hotel ballroom to cheers and applause from fancy dressed people sitting at small round tables. In the dim light of the room, they would shout "More!" and "One more song!" The lyrics of Bessie Smith's "My Kitchen Man" would be too off-color for those high-class folks, but I thought of Charlie as my own kitchen man and laughed out loud about the kitchen man's jelly roll Bessie sang about. I preferred Charlie's sausage—nice and spicy. I sang songs I had heard in speakeasies with Floyd, like "Saint Louis Blues" about a woman set to pack up her things and move to Missouri. I'd never been to Saint Louis, but Charlie and I had made deliveries all the way to Louisville. One day I thought we might keep going and see what was on the other side of the Mississippi River.

The reward for tiring nights of driving was a pocketful of cash, a warm bath, a hot meal, a few shots of whiskey, and my skin against Charlie's smooth skin, naked as newborns, loving each other until past early dawn.

One cloudy night in late autumn, I left the filling station under a drizzle, a good evening for piloting deliveries because the sheriff's deputies were less likely to be out by the barricades. If they waited in a car, I'd have no problem outrunning them because the Ford was light and fast. But tonight the wipers were sluggish and rain on the windscreen blurred whatever I saw in the headlamps. I took my foot off the gas and drifted to fifty—no point sliding into a ditch on a slick road.

It was then I heard the voice. "Slow down, Willie." It sounded like May's voice. "Slow down. Watch the road."

"I did slow down, damn it!" I said aloud.

"Slooow dooown," the voice said again. I pushed my hair behind an ear. I must've been hearing things—the growl of the engine, rain on the Ford's roof.

Ahead, I saw what looked to be a face with brown curly hair like my mother's, distorted and wavy through the wet glass. Was it May? No, the voice was inside the car, not on the road. I had five-dollar bills in my pocket to pay my way through a barricade if it came to that, but I didn't see a copper car—only a small brown object alone in the road.

An animal?

By now I was doing thirty and could swerve around whatever it was—raccoon? Fox? It might have been rabid standing stupidly in the road under rain that came down harder by the minute.

I pressed on the horn, but the animal didn't move. Could have been a trap federal agent Sam White had set. Samuel O. White was his full name. He was bound and determined to shut down the whiskey business and especially bent on shutting down Willie Carter Sharpe. But he wouldn't get me even for reckless driving at that speed.

Finally I stomped on the brake, stopping the Ford feet from the animal.

"Damned if it isn't a dog," I said. It was small, probably young, shivering in the cold. The dog looked at me through the windscreen, our eyes meeting.

"What're you doing in the road after midnight, you fool thing?" I said as if the dog could hear me.

It was not wise to sit there with the law prowling the area, but I couldn't leave a mutt on the motorway either. I shifted into neutral, set the brake and got out, leaving the engine running. Scanning the area, I searched for a nearby house with lights on or any building the dog might have come from, but fog hovered over fields on both sides of the road and I couldn't see far. No lights anywhere.

Slowly I approached, half expecting the dog to attack. It didn't have on a collar, but it wasn't in a defensive crouch like a wild thing.

"What's going on, boy?" I said. "You hurt?"

The dog lay down, looked up at me with big brown eyes, and thumped its tail. It appeared to be sound, just bony and scared.

"Somebody abandon you, fella?" It was probably trying to find its way home, and rain on the pavement could confuse the scent.

"Look, boy," I said, "we got to get out of here, you and me both." I took another look around but didn't see other vehicles in either direction. "How about you get in with me? At least it's warmer in the car than out here." If it intended to bite me, I'd rather it not chase me down the road.

Beagle size but wirehaired, the dog's paws showed it was probably not full grown. Lucky to be a year old.

A foreign instinct wrapped around my heart. If I didn't know better, I'd think it had to do with nurturing. I knew I had to take care of this pup.

"C'mon, now," I said. The dog got to its feet and followed me to the Ford. When I opened the door, it jumped in as if it had been accustomed to leaping into cars.

"Okay then," I said. "Guess I've got me a copilot."

The pistons whined and we rolled forward. Less than two hundred yards ahead, the dog snarled. I reached over and it let me pat its head.

"Easy, boy," I crooned. The dog settled for a minute and then stood and planted its front paws on the dashboard. Whatever it sensed, I wasn't able make out through the fogged-up glass. Suddenly the dog barked, growled, and barked again. Adrenaline rushed through my veins. Probably a mistake picking up the pup. Something seemed to be haunting it, something unpleasant.

"You been through tough times, boy?" I considered opening the door and putting it out in the rain again. Whatever was bothering the dog was none of my business.

When I could see out the windscreen, I caught sight of lights at the top of the hill—bright lights. Headlamps. At least three sets of them. Cars in the middle of the night in the middle of the road meant only one thing.

I switched off the headlamps and slowed. The fog was thinner at the bottom of the hill and I didn't want to risk being seen.

"Hold on, boy," I said and jerked the wheel, fishtailing the Ford into a one-eighty. The dog slammed against the passenger door and yelped. When we straightened out, he shook himself, and I switched on the lights and hit the gas pedal. I'd have to find another way to lead Charlie to Harrisonburg.

Charlie was coming up behind me. He must have seen the Ford because he pulled over and turned around. Route 11 was a thoroughfare, which was why the law wouldn't be looking there. They'd suspect we'd take back roads. During the Civil War the route was the main road through the Shenandoah Valley. Rebel soldiers blocked it off to keep the Union army from coming through and destroying fields. The Valley was the breadbasket for the southern troops and if the Union couldn't defeat the Rebels in battle, they'd try to starve them to death by running their wagons through crops of corn and grain.

Eleven was a risk I was willing to take.

"Hope we haven't run ourselves into hell itself, boy," I said to the dog but as we got close to Harrisonburg, hell was creeping up on me in the form of a copper car.

I slowed down and the copper waved me over.

This officer must have been new. I didn't recognize him. He came to the window wearing a dark blue uniform, rain dripping from the bill of his hat.

When I rolled down the window, the dog nearly jumped over me to get at the man.

"Keep your dog under control," he said.

"Yes, sir," I responded and wrapped an arm around the dog's neck. It growled a warning at the officer.

"You seem in a hurry, ma'am," he said. "I followed you at seventy. Have any identification?"

"No, sir," I said. "My name's Mildred—Mildred Mackey. Sorry to be speeding, but I've got an emergency on my hands and forgot my identification."

"What sort of emergency?" he said.

I kept talking, talking my way out of an arrest. The pup helped. "See, this dog's got an abscess and hasn't been able to eat for days. I've got to get him to the animal hospital before he starves to death."

The dog showed its teeth.

"Hunger makes a dog mean," I said.

"They expecting you in Harrisonburg?"

"Yes," I said. "I called ahead and the vet is meeting us at the office."

"Well, then, Miss Mackey—"

"Mrs. Mackey." I didn't want any foolishness tonight, not with the dog. I wasn't sure what it might do.

The officer knocked on the Ford's roof.

"Let you go this time, but don't let it happen again," he said. "Wouldn't want you and your pet to get into an accident."

I rolled up the window and released the dog's neck. "Thanks, boy," I said. "Think I'll call you Hooch." I ruffled its neck fur. "That okay with you?"

The dog panted happily.

Through the back window I could see Charlie's truck pulled over, lights off as if he had parked.

I waited until the copper pulled ahead of us. He must have been on the local force in Harrisonburg. Whether Charlie's load was meant for students at the State Teachers College, their professors, or a secret watering hole, I figured we'd gotten him there, thanks to Hooch.

The dog nosed my arm again.

"We did good, huh, boy?"

Hooch licked my hand.

•　　•　　•

Late that night, I pulled the Ford behind the Blackwater station and waited for Charlie to return. Lights were still on at the 24-hour place, but anybody meaning to do business had gone off somewhere.

Charlie pulled in and came to meet me at the car.

"Let's get you home and warm you up," he said.

"Both of us?" I opened the door and Hooch sprang over me and landed in Charlie's arms.

"What in the Sam Hill?" Charlie said.

"Guess you could say this straggler adopted me." I got out of the car and petted the dog in his arms. "I'm calling him Hooch—you know, Hooch the pooch."

Charlie held the dog up and in the faint glow regarded it.

"Well," he said, "Hoochie-Coochie would be a better name. This fella is a female."

I planted a hand on my hip. "Why would anyone leave such a sweet girl in the middle of nowhere?"

"Females are a problem," Charlie said, "unless you want to breed them. Expensive to neuter and if you don't, you'll have a lapful of pups to deal with." He winked at me. "Males are easier. Clip, clip and you're good to go."

"Except for humping everything."

"Not all males—some of us hump only one female at a time." Charlie grinned. "Now let's get you two out of here."

At the bungalow Coochie ate a bowl of Charlie's scrapple and some bread with peanut butter and drank her fill of water. That night and the nights that followed she slept at the foot of our bed and rode out the rocking and tumbling of her new masters. I heard the pup sigh when things finally settled down.

Coochie came with me most nights I piloted. I was afraid she'd hurt herself if I had to do a quick turnaround or take a sharp curve at high speed, but Coochie was surefooted. Most of the time she stay curled up on the seat, one ear up on alert. If we got stopped at a barricade, she growled, but when I passed a sawbuck out the window to move the obstruction, she settled down again.

On rare nights off for resting up from deliveries, Charlie and I walked Coochie to Elmwood Park for some exercise. Without fail, if a lawman's car drove by, Coochie started barking. Whatever it was she had against police officers, sheriff's deputies, and federal agents remained a mystery, but I was glad to have her warning signal.

15.
Jimmy — 1929

From watching Pop, I knew about making moonshine. His still was in a shed out behind the barn. At one point the building might have served for spare parts for farm equipment — bale spears, blade shanks, hitch pin, rake tines, bailing twine — things like that. But he cleaned it out, moved the parts into the barn, and set up his still. Mountain men built big stills in the woods along paths overgrown with briars and poison ivy to discourage snooping federal agents. Those stills were for major production of liquor, but Pop's was such a small operation agents must have figured it wasn't worth sending him to jail. They went after the big producers. Most of those makers spent some time behind bars — thrown to the dogs they called it. After a few weeks locked up, they came out to cook up more juice. The money was good, and prison was like a vacation — rest, room, and board.

A distiller had to be smart enough to know how the equipment worked — the mash fermenter, boiler, worm pipe, and slobber bucket. Copper was the best metal because it didn't leach into the alcohol. He had to keep everything clean, preferably sterilized, and connected with a sealer you could eat — not lead, which could make you go blind or insane. Good moonshine like Pop's was made with barley, corn, yeast, and spring water. Fermentation happens when the yeast breaks down the corn into sugar, but if you want gallons you can sell fast, add more sugar than corn or replace the corn entirely with sugar. Franklin County moonshine was in high demand, and cargo trains dropped off fifty-pound bags of sugar for the distillers. A good maker would add barley for flavor, but large producers left it out altogether. A moonshiner could make two bucks a day, enough to keep the household running but not enough to get rich or wear diamond tie clips like the dealers.

Moonshine is meant to be imbibed right away. Aging caused evaporation, and evaporation was like money disappearing into the air. May kept three corked gallons in the bottom of the old oak ice box. She flavored each one with whatever was in season. One was infused with spring blueberries, one with summer peaches, and the third with fall plums. She said if she kept them sitting for a few months, she'd have brandy, which was more palatable than that harsh liquor Pop made. I tasted the blueberry brandy, and it wasn't too bad. But men who want to drink don't want to wait.

There is a chemistry to making moonshine. I watched Pop catch the first drips in a small jar and toss it into the bushes. "Foreshot," he called it. The foreshot contains most of the methanol from the mash and can paralyze or kill you. Pop ran his batch twice or sometimes three times through the still to filter out the impurities. Neighbors often stopped by to see when his next batch would be ready and if he had a quart or two, he'd hand it over for a fair price. They said his whiskey was the best in the county and he could be a rich man if he'd build a bigger still. He didn't drink all that much and considered it his medicine for aches and pains and a sleep elixir. I couldn't recall ever seeing him staggering drunk. May wouldn't have allowed it.

16.
Willie — 1929

I was careful when I drank liquor. If I drank too much, I got reflective about what I might have become besides an outlaw hiding from federal agents. Herbert Hoover himself was born in a two-room shack and was left an orphan when he was young. Yet he found his way to college and had the audacity to run for public office. Becoming President of the United States had been an ambition even too big for him. He had lowered taxes, but I saw firsthand the gap getting wider between the haves and the have-nots. He hadn't fixed that, and I sensed the worst was yet to come.

When Charlie drank, he was less careful. Drinking made him happy. He liked the song "In the Jailhouse Now" and sang it holding up a wooden spoon like a microphone while he and Coochie danced around the kitchen, Charlie substituting some of the words about Ramblin' Bob for Charlie and his gal. I didn't think the jailhouse was a joke and asked him to stop, which only encouraged him. On nights when he'd had a little too much of the local brew, I helped him into bed and he fell asleep with his head on my shoulder like a little boy. Those nights I started to feel old, as if I was taking care of a teenager. Charlie was two years younger than I was and made a point to stay under the radar, although he had spent a few nights in the jailhouse himself.

High-speed piloting was a different story. There were nights on a piloting mission when the speed, the headlamps slicing razor beams into the darkness, brought me to whoop with excitement. But some nights I drifted into a tranquil space when it seemed the car was driving itself. I knew the roads and I almost believed the Ford had a mind and had learned them, too. On one of those nights, I steered into a sharp curve so fast the vehicle leaned to the left, the tires on the right, rear and front, lifted from the ground and I steered with only the two wheels still on the road. For a moment, I thought I had taken flight, a heron, wings outstretched. Time slowed to the seconds between life and death. Then time stopped altogether and I remembered the story I heard of a father who took his son on a camping trip. During the night a panther attacked the boy, gripping the boy's head in its powerful jaws. The boy cried out and the father jumped to his feet, felt for his rifle. Still drowsy, he had grabbed the barrel instead of the stock and struck the panther with the rifle butt again and again until the big cat released his son whose head and face were sticky with blood. Days later, the boy, recovering from a cracked skull, told his father he had not been afraid but had been surrounded by a sense of peace, as if no harm would come to him. I had the same sense of peace, the Ford tilted on two wheels or no wheels at all as I flew. Was I controlling the automobile or had a heavenly hand come down to right it without causing me a speck of harm?

Coochie barked her warning when I had a close call like that one. When the four wheels slammed onto the road, I found my breath and remembered my job, my task of controlling the car, of keeping Charlie Sharpe safe from the sheriff's deputies.

"We've got a handle on this, girl," I told Coochie.

Later — before daybreak — I would be in Charlie's bed again, his arms around me, and the sense of wellbeing returned. For those hours with Charlie, the risk was worth everything. I'd have driven around the world, eluded every pursuer to have again and again the magic I felt with Charlie Sharpe.

Within the next year I had cleared Charlie to carry thousands of gallons of bootleg liquor up the east coast, sometimes to the same address two or three times a week. Speakeasies, private parties, back doors of mansions, and shop stockrooms. Our clients were rich or not so rich, the celebrated and the anonymous. Our reputation had grown so that the Sharpes were the law's target in every county in Virginia, West Virginia, and eastern Kentucky—which for me meant driving faster and with trickier moves.

One starry summer night at the Blackwater station, while Charlie loaded the truck with jars of liquor, I checked the Ford's engine. Air intake—clean. All eight spark plugs seated and secure. Oil a little low, so I topped it off, careful not to overfill. I reminded myself to replace the filter with a clean one tomorrow. Like most southerners, I was opposed to the Eighteenth Amendment. Except for speed and fancy driving, I didn't think of my employment as law breaking. Citizens had been making and drinking their own moonshine since the caveman era. The Declaration of Independence was written over Thomas Jefferson's ale and pewter cups of whiskey from George Washington's own distillery. In fact, General Washington had stills set up beside Revolutionary War campsites to raise soldiers' spirits—with his own spirits. During the Civil War, women worked the stills and carried jugs of their whiskey to their fighting men. It made no sense to me why the U.S. government would kowtow to a temperance movement run by a group of women who carped about their drunken husbands. I believed everything in moderation— everything except when it came to driving—and loving. When Charlie and I met up in the early morning hours, it was food, love-making, a few hours of sleep, more loving, mapping the night's escapade, and refining the engines at Blackwater.

I walked around the Ford, checked the tires and they looked in good condition. I turned on the lights — nothing amiss there. We were raking in good money, and my mind drifted to things I could buy. I had packed a closet with dresses and shoes, furs and jewels, even imagined getting a country house with Charlie, maybe a toddler padding over the polished wood floors. But living outside the present was careless. Every cell of my body, every spark in my brain had to be focused on the machine, the road, and keeping my man safe from the law. My dreams had changed to make room for a partner. But for now and for the sake of prosperity and survival, those dreams would stay locked in the future. I was about to lead the law on a chase that would rattle even a wild goose.

It was prudent to steer clear of Charlie before the night's run. He was a distraction — albeit an appealing one. If I thought about his smooth chest, his sinewy arms, his manhood standing at attention summoning me, my mind would wander. One day we would drive together in a fine car — a Cadillac — but tonight I felt the tingle of speed calling me. And like a switch, I turned out one light and turned on another.

But then Charlie walked over to the Ford.

"You won't be driving tonight," he said.

"What? Of course I'm driving." Something must have happened he hadn't told me about. "Anything wrong with the truck?"

"The truck's fine. But I've got a bad feeling about tonight."

"A feeling?" I raised my eyebrows. "Where exactly is this feeling you're having?"

"Willie, we're going into Kentucky."

"I know. Ashland. Not far over the border."

"The revenuers have a reputation for meanness there," he said. "They're out for us, and I don't want to risk you getting hurt."

"Out for us doesn't mean they'll get us."

"I said I'll handle this load alone."

When he started to turn around, I grabbed his sleeve.

"Why is it men think they have the privilege of telling me what they think I should do?" I let go of his jacket and lifted my arms. "These hands, these feet do what this head tells them. And this head—" I tapped my temple. "It says I'm going to drive this automobile tonight." I opened the driver's door. "So if you'll kindly move your caboose out of the way, I'll get on with it."

I cranked the engine. Charlie didn't try to stop me as I slid behind the wheel.

"All right," he said, "but Coochie's coming with me."

Slobber dripped from the dog's tongue. I reckoned giving up Coochie was a concession I'd have to make if I intended to drive that night. But Coochie was my good luck charm. That night I guessed I'd have to make my own luck.

Slowly I pulled onto the road, seeing no need to rush until I caught sight of the law. Like football, Charlie and I were a team, the revenuers the opposition. The teams weren't enemies—both of us were just doing our jobs. There was no animosity—only loyalty to our own sides. And I didn't like my loyalty to Charlie being brought into question, not even by Charlie himself.

The quickest way to Ashland was up to Blacksburg and then northwest. I'd have to climb some mountains to get over the Blue Ridge, burning gasoline. Why Kentucky yokels didn't pour their own moonshine down their throats must have had to do with the better quality and taste of Virginia's product. I'd heard some Kentuckians had gone blind from drinking bad hooch, but Charlie said he was delivering to a special breed— probably judges and lawyers who couldn't risk patronizing their own homegrown liquor—physically or politically.

It was a four-and-a-half-hour leisurely drive to Ashland. I could cut that to two and a half if the Ford's fuel held out, and I shouldn't have to gas up again until Ashland. That would put me almost on the Ohio border, too close for comfort to Chicago mobster territory, and nobody messed with Al Capone. This past February he had gunned down seven bootleg rivals in broad daylight in what came to be known as the Saint Valentine's Day massacre. I hoped old Scarface wasn't setting us up for an ambush.

As it turned out, Capone was the last thing I had to worry about. I was almost to the West Virginia line and making my way through Giles County when I sensed lights coming up behind the Ford. Anything moving that fast had to be either a meteor or the law. I snapped my head around to see whether a lawman was hanging out the window with a pistol in his hand. If he had me in his sights, the bullets would have to hit a moving target.

"Come on, come on—a little closer," I growled. When they were near enough to unload lead at me, I made a sharp turn and headed toward downtown Pearisburg. Passing closed shops and diners, I careened down Main Street and wove through narrow side streets like threading a needle. Without dropping a stitch, I downshifted, revved the engine, and heard the tires squeal.

As I approached the edge of the small town, I spotted the federal agents' car stopped across the road ahead. If I couldn't shake them, I'd scare hell out of them. Barreling toward the bullseye, I intended to swerve onto the sidewalk and avoid a collision, but when I pumped the brakes, the Ford didn't answer. When was the last time I'd checked the pads and rotors? I hadn't thought about slowing down. The job was about speed, not pussyfooting.

Seconds before I rammed into the side of the agents' car, I spotted two men inside, hands up to their faces as if trying to stop the oncoming disaster. I jerked the wheel and squeezed my eyes shut. The impact jolted the Ford to a stop, but my head hit something—maybe the steering wheel. I raised my head up and saw the agents' car start to roll in slow motion and tumble like a fat man turning over in bed.

Some liquid trickled down my forehead. When I wiped it away, I saw a smear of dark red on my hand. Must have hit my head harder than I thought. The windscreen glass wasn't cracked. I wasn't so sure about my skull.

My first thought was relief Coochie wasn't with me. Charlie's premonition was on the mark. I hoped he and Cooch were going to make it to Ashland without a scratch.

Stumbling out of the Ford, I saw the front end had only a scrape in the black paint, thanks to Charlie's work at reinforcing the chassis with steel. The law's car was another story. It lay on its roof, its wheels spinning like an upturned beetle, legs running through the air.

Deputy Sheriff Lewis Bridges was struggling to climb out a broken window on the passenger side.

"You all right, Sheriff?" I said.

"Yeah," he answered, "I believe I'm in one piece. Help me get Sam out."

Together we peeled Sam White out the driver's side and laid him on the ground, careful not to shake the car unless it decided to make another revolution.

I inspected White, whose arm lay at a crooked angle.

"Arm's broken, I expect," I said. "Other than that, I think you're okay."

White glared at me. "Most bootleggers would have taken to the woods. What'd you stick around for?"

"I was about to ask myself the same question. I'm hoping you'll pin a medal of honor on me."

White spoke to Bridges. "Put her under arrest for carrying and distributing illegal alcohol."

"You won't find any whiskey in that car," I said.

The sheriff limped to the Ford, opened the doors, jerked open the trunk.

"Hope you're satisfied," I said.

"You're piloting, aren't you?" Bridges said.

"Just out for a joy ride."

A pie wagon roared toward the wreck, a panel truck made for hauling Christmas pies as well as crooks and troublemakers. In the eyes of the law I was a troublemaker. I hoped the seats were comfortable.

"Looks like you've had a heap of trouble here," the driver said.

"Evening, John," Bridges said. "I'd say that's about right."

White struggled to his feet. "We can get her for reckless driving and eluding officers of the law."

"You gentlemen are outside your territory, aren't you?" I said.

"Willie, I don't think Sheriff Adair will mind escorting us to Franklin County, will you, John?" Bridges pulled my left arm behind my back and locked my wrist in a metal cuff. I didn't resist when he did the same to my right wrist.

"On account of the lateness of the night and the condition of your vehicle, I'd prefer you handle this situation on your own turf," Adair said. "Put her in the wagon." He nodded toward his vehicle. "You boys climb aboard, too, and we'll drop Mr. White at the hospital."

"Sorry about this, Willie," Bridges said, "but you're not going to be getting behind the wheel again for a good long time." He pushed me to the rear of Adair's truck.

17.
Jimmy — 1929

I wasn't surprised to get a letter from Willie sent from the Roanoke County jail saying her trial date was a week away and she'd be behind bars until then. The sheriff had given her a roll of toilet paper for two uses, wiping and using as a pillow. Her sarcasm came across when she wrote the jail was on the top floor of the courthouse where she had married Floyd Carter. That day she should have seen the writing on the wall.

Pop and I went to Willie's trial. He was wearing his best fedora, a white shirt, vest, and his only tie. I supposed he meant to present himself as a respectable, law-abiding father. Pop said if his daughter was in trouble, he'd do everything he could to get her out of it. But I couldn't see Pop going up against the Virginia state legal system. May said she didn't want her heart broken and stayed to tend the farm.

We sat as far forward as we could get without breathing down her court-appointed lawyer's neck. Pro bono, Pop called him, which meant Willie couldn't pay the fee for a real attorney, at least not with her moonshine money. There was no jury. A Roanoke judge listened to testimony from two law officers, one of them Sheriff Bridges, before he fired questions at Willie.

"How old are you, Mrs. Sharpe?" the judge asked.

How old was she now? Twenty-four? Or would that be her next birthday? She told him twenty-five. With a baby and a wife, I had missed a year.

He asked about the Ford, about why she was out at that time of night. The Ford belonged to a friend who'd given her permission to use it, she said. She had trouble sleeping and was joy riding late at night when there was no traffic on the roads. So how could driving fast be reckless?

Was she delivering moonshine?

"There was not a drop of liquor in the car, as Sheriff Bridges testified," she said.

"How fast were you driving before you hit the sheriff's vehicle?"

"I had to slow down to under a hundred coming through town," she said.

"Under a hundred? the judge asked. "Miles an hour?"

I felt my neck muscles tense up. Willie had said the wrong thing. I'd never been in a vehicle going that speed and I doubted the judge had either. It would've been better to tell him she had no idea how fast she was going. But I saw her swear to tell nothing but the truth, and Willie was a woman of her word.

"Miles an hour, yes, sir."

"And how fast were you going when you hit the sheriff's car?"

She could have told him ninety and it wouldn't have been a lie. But she said, "The brakes failed, sir."

The judge grimaced and pushed papers around on his desk. Deputy Sheriff Bridges must have seen her headlights coming at him. He was probably too frozen with surprise to get his car into gear and stalled the engine. Like the summer I jumped from a ledge into the Lick Fork River without checking for depth. I saw the big rock too late, but you can't stop gravity.

Pop made me do chores with that sprained ankle—broke probably, but he said it's what I got for stupidity.

I held in a laugh to think of Bridges chasing Willie and next thing he knows, Willie is bearing down on him, not meaning to, but no room to get around the sheriff's car without veering into the plate glass window of the millinery shop. She would yank the wheel to the right, spinning the Ford, its rear end catching hard against the sheriff's vehicle. The way Willie described it, I could hear the awful crunching sound, Bridges's auto teetering up on two wheels like a drunkard, him grabbing the window frame as he rose with the car.

"Were you hurt?" the judge asked.

"Had a sharp pain in my side and blood dribbling down my face." She dabbed at her forehead with a hanky as if remembering the tickle of blood.

The judge clicked his tongue. "It's lucky all three of you weren't killed."

It took him less than a minute to pronounce it advisable to keep one Willie Carter Sharpe off the roads and away from sober, God-fearing folks. Three years in the Washington, DC house of detention for women and children.

Three years—and she wasn't carrying liquor.

Pop stood up. His lips moved as if to protest the sentence, but he held his tongue. A judge's declaration was law, and the law was law.

After the sentencing, officers shackled Willie's ankles and wrists. It broke my heart to see her treated that way.

18.
Willie — 1929

Washington was brutal in August. Through the small window I watched heat rise from the sidewalk, causing the air to ripple like looking through old glass. The cherry and apple blossoms had rendered their fruit, and it splattered on the ground like drops of blood. The fermenting smell made me feel drunk, and I'd have given an arm and a leg for some of that hooch Charlie and I used to drink.

When I first arrived, the building looked like a huge rectangle of stone taking up a city block. Squeals of children came from a fenced side yard, poor souls stuck in the same jail with their mothers because they had no other place to go. But they looked to be making the most of it. The prison couldn't be too bad with young'uns playing happily nearby.

I had been in the prison for three months when Jimmy took the train to pay me a visit. A warden led him upstairs and down a hall of locked cells, each holding a woman looking forlorn but not dangerous. I'd come to know them all. One bit her nails. Another sang hymns nonstop. Others flipped through magazines or dozed most of the time.

When an officer admitted Jimmy to my cell, he looked stunned to see me in the same uniform as the other women — floppy blouse of horizontal stripes over a skirt with up-and-down stripes and sitting on a narrow cot, mattress covered with a thin sheet. Did he expect I'd be wearing my best duds and relaxing on a Recamier sofa like the one I had at Floyd's house?

"Jimmy," I said without smiling. I'd always made the best of a bad situation, but the months in prison had taken the joy from my soul.

"You doing okay, Willie?" he asked.

I shrugged. "Meals are served regular right to the bars of the door." I shrugged again. "Reckon I shouldn't complain. They let us out once a day so we can sit at those little desks." I nodded to school desks lined up down the center of the hallway like a classroom. "They give us books to read. Trying to reform us into upstanding citizens."

"I don't remember you reading books before," he said.

"Not much else to do in here. With your high school diploma, you've probably digested a lot of those books on the prison shelf." I looked through the bars at the bookcase. "I'm working my way through *Heart of Darkness* where this fellow Kurtz—English, I think—is a kind of god to the African natives," I said.

"My hat's off to you. I wasn't able to get through Conrad's book," Jimmy said.

"I feel like Kurtz in this place." I turned my head from side to side. "These women think I'm some kind of saint because I tried to kill a lawman." I pointed a finger at him. "That's hogwash, and you know it."

"Hogwash that you're a saint? Or that you tried to kill the sheriff?"

I punched his arm—hard. "You know I wouldn't kill my worst enemy, Jimmy."

"That's true. I can't recall you ever being cruel to man or beast. But wasn't that federal agent your worst enemy?"

"I wouldn't say enemy. Antagonist is a better word." I gave him a smirk. "How's that for building up my vocabulary?"

"Looks like you've found a sense of humor since you've been in here," he said.

"To be honest, being isolated suits me as well as driving alone in the middle of the night. I don't fit anywhere else — not on the farm and not in law-abiding society." I leaned against the bars. "Guess I have an ache in me and a need to ease it by driving fast or rubbing the law the wrong way and getting away with it."

"I can't comprehend what pain haunts you, Willie, and I don't know how to help you get loose from it, but I'll always be a brother to you, no matter what trouble you get into."

I admit I got choked up, but I didn't want Jimmy to see me shed tears. I thought it wise to change the subject.

"How old are you now, Jimmy?" I said.

"Twenty-two. You knew I was married, didn't you?"

"Yeah. And kids, too." I tapped his belly. "Looks like Dottie's feeding you well."

"We're doing fine." He stepped to the window and looked through the bars. "At least you can watch traffic — more cars than horses now."

I got up and stood by the window next to him. "That's Ohio and Fifteenth," I said. "I itch when I see those clumsy drivers blunder their vehicles through the stop sign."

"Say — when you get out you ought to open a driving school."

"Ha," I chortled. "A criminal teaching upstanding citizens how to operate their expensive machinery?" I crooked my head toward the hallway. "Wouldn't get much business unless it was from these wayward women."

"You're like a tiger in a cage, Willie," he said.

I shook my head and pushed a strand of hair from my cheek.

"More like a cheetah in a leg-hold." I tried to smile but failed. Then I looked my brother square in the eyes. "I sure miss Coochie—and Charlie, too, and I'd gnaw off a limb if it would get me out of this place."

When a uniformed guard led two women down the hallway, they stopped at my cell door.

"Willie Carter Sharpe, two more visitors," he said, unlocking the door. "Ten minutes." He held the door and looked at Jimmy as if to say his time was up.

"Curtis," I said, "this here's my little brother. Blood relatives don't have a time limit."

He probably rankled at being called little. Jimmy stood above me by a couple inches and may not have finished growing yet.

Curtis pulled his mouth to the side. "All right, Sharpe," he said. "But only ten minutes more."

Jimmy leaned into a corner, and the guard stood aside for two women to enter the cell.

"Hey, Willie, remember us?"

"Juanita," I said. "Damn."

Juanita had on a pretty cotton dress and wide-brimmed hat. My hand went to my own tangle of hair, and I thought of the silks hanging in the closet at Charlie's place, silks it would be a couple more years before I'd be able to get into. I folded my arms over my chest as if to hide the prison garb I had to wear.

Ethel followed Juanita in looking as if she had coordinated her outfit with Juanita's. Where did they think they were going—to church?

When the guard closed the gate behind them, I said, "Bring in a silver service of tea for me and my guests, will you, Curtis?"

The guard smirked. "Sure, Sharpe."

The ladies stood surveying my small confinement.

"You gals remember my brother Jimmy?" I said.

"Hello, Jimmy," Juanita said. "I thought you were called Junebug."

He winced. "Not since I was yay high."

I sat on the bunk and patted the mattress next to me for Juanita. Ethel chose the metal chair, the only other furniture. She sucked in a breath and forced a smile.

"You're a celebrity, Willie," she said. "Everybody's talking about you and your fancy driving. People were taking odds on whether the police would ever catch you."

"They didn't catch me," I said. "I caught them. You'd think they'd have thrown a party to thank me."

Juanita laughed. "Willie, you haven't changed a bit."

"Lost some weight. They serve better food on pig farms." I swiveled my head between the two women. "Looks like you gals've done pretty well for yourselves. Keeping your noses clean, I reckon."

"I married a preacher," Juanita said. "Guess it's in my blood." She turned to Ethel. "Ethel here, she's still looking."

What did I have to look forward to? My first husband was a dud. And look where my second marriage landed me.

"How's Lois?" I asked. I'd gotten a letter from her, but she hadn't mentioned Charlie.

"Lois has a playpen full of kids and a husband who keeps her on a short leash," Juanita said.

"Good for her," I said. "I thought she'd come to no good trying to break into the bright lights."

There was a pause in the conversation which must have made Ethel uncomfortable. Her hand went to her neck and she scanned the tin can that was now my abode.

"How long're you in for, Willie?" she asked.

I laced my fingers together and pressed them between my knees. "Judge gave me three years." I glared at Ethel and raised my voice. "Three years for reckless driving? There's nothing reckless about my driving and they know it."

"There ought to be a law against an unfair sentence like that," Ethel said.

"A bird flies free and its spirit soars with it," I said. "Put it in a cage, and its spirit flies away. Not that the judge cares about anybody's spirit." I looked toward the high window. "Anyway, expect I'll get out sooner if I behave myself."

In an awkward moment, Juanita looked up at the window. Jimmy buried a single cough in his fist. Ethel shifted on the chair. Both ladies knew the question I wanted to ask—the question that had burned in my heart for the past weeks.

"Any of you seen Charlie?" I willed my voice not to quaver. "I wrote him half a dozen letters and not a single word. Is he still delivering the goods or is he locked up like me?"

Ethel stared at Juanita. It took a few seconds for Juanita to answer.

"You know how it is—in his business."

"Yeah, I guess I do," I said. "But if you run into him, tell him to come pay me a visit."

"Sure, Willie." Juanita forced a smile.

Ethel brightened enough to change the subject. "Say, Willie—I'm a floor manager at Woolworth's now, and my girls can't believe I know the famous Willie Carter Sharpe. They say you've got diamonds set in your teeth. Is that true?"

"Your friends sure have an imagination." I smiled so they could see the tiny diamond embedded in my front tooth."

"I thought that gossip was pure embroidery," Ethel said. "But you always had a penchant for glamor, Willie."

"Everybody's calling you the rum-running queen," Juanita said. "Ain't that something?"

"That's something, all right." I opened my arms. "Welcome to my palace."

Ethel leaned forward on the metal chair. "Do you think when you get out of here I could ride with you one night?"

I pulled my mouth to one side. "I'm done driving. If I ever get out, I'm going on the up and up."

"I can't see you going back to being a cigar counter clerk," Juanita said.

"How will you get along, Willie?" Ethel asked.

Her question rankled me. I wasn't sure myself how I'd get along. Working on Pop's farm? I didn't want to go backwards, but how could I go forward with a name it seemed like everyone knew? I thought of outlaws like Billy the Kid, a cattle rustler, robber, and murderer. Jesse James fought for the Confederates in the Civil War and later robbed trains and banks to support his wife and children. Both outlaws came to violent ends. But I hadn't robbed anyone and I certainly hadn't killed anyone. Yet here I was, serving time for undermining a law that should never have been passed.

"I have my wits," I said. "I'll always find a way."

Curtis appeared and opened the cell door. "Time's up, ladies — gentleman," he said.

Juanita stood and bent to kiss me on the cheek. "Well, you take care now, Willie Carter Sharpe."

"You too." I shook a finger at each of the women. "And stay away from the hooch. I hear that stuff's real bad for you."

"Aw, Willie," Juanita said.

After they left, I turned to Jimmy. "You'll be all right, won't you, brother?"

"Don't worry about me," he said. "I kept going to that dilapidated schoolhouse like you said until I got the piece of paper they handed out. Pop made a frame and put it on the wall."

"I'm sure proud of you." I hated to see him go. Jimmy was one of the best things about me. No matter how much trouble I'd had, I could always count on him. "You give those boys of yours a kiss from their Aunt Willie."

When he reached his arms around me and gave me a good hug, it was all I could do to hold back the tears.

"You take care of yourself, Wilhelmina Collins," he whispered.

I'd never heard him say my full name before. I guess he wanted me to remember who I was and where I came from — good, clean people who asked for nothing they couldn't grow or earn themselves. People who stood by their own and tried their best to do right.

After he left, I looked around my prison cell. It seemed like my branch had fallen off the family tree.

19.
Jimmy – 1930

When the prison released Willie, I waited for her train to arrive at the Roanoke station. I'd been working two jobs and made enough to buy a motorcar, nothing fancy, just a two-seater with enough room for a satchel.

By the train station, the new Roanoke Hotel occupied a city block and five stories of airspace. Like everywhere else, Roanoke had fallen into hard times. The press called it a depression. People lost their jobs, banks closed taking investors' life savings with them, and families went hungry. Out-of-work folks gathered chestnuts from under trees, and farmers helped each other out in exchange for a noon dinner. But there always seemed to be money for whiskey.

Pop's arm never was the same, and he was slowing down. Although he begrudged help from the neighbors, he knew working the farm was keeping him alive – if by a thread. May canned everything that grew, even sausage and chicken, and stored the jars in a cool place under the porch. I never saw her eat much, though. She was shrunken and held one hand perpetually under her breasts. Although she didn't complain, the grimace that marked her face told me she was in pain. I had asked Dottie about moving to the farm with the kids to help take care of May, but she said she'd never be happy doing the drudgery of a farm wife and recommended Pop hire some help.

In spite of the Prohibition law and the risk of ending up in handcuffs, I kept a jar of Pop's moonshine at our place in the bottom cupboard, which had a lock on it. I'd never acquired much of a taste for the clear liquid, but Dottie let me keep it for special occasions. She even had a nip mixed with prune juice on New Year's Eve, both of which gave her the runs and ruined our chance of getting the New Year off to a favorable start.

I shook regrets from my mind when Willie came out of a rail car looking fresh and wearing a simple cotton dress the prison must have given her. No mink stole, no Italian leather shoes. She'd lost weight and the spark I remembered when we were kids was gone.

"Where to?" I asked when she was in the car. I was surprised she wasn't set on driving.

"I've been writing Lois. She lives up near Hanging Rock, by the college," she said, her focus steady through the windshield. "Take me there."

When we got to Lois's cottage, Willie told me to wait in the car, she wouldn't be long. I figured she had one objective—to find Charlie Sharpe. And Lois knew his whereabouts.

Willie returned ten minutes later.

"Those kids are cute as I expected," she said, "but they make a racket and pull on Lo's apron strings." There was a sad note to her voice. She looked older than her twenty-six years, the age when she should have been settling down and having kids of her own instead of finishing a stint in prison.

When a silence fell between us, I watched her pat the neat waves about her cheeks.

"You want to go see him, don't you." It wasn't a question.

She turned her head away said, "Lo gave me the address."

When we found the house, Willie was out of the car before I shifted into neutral. She walked up the steps to the stoop wearing a hat Dottie would say was out of style by a couple years. Her knuckles rose to knock on the oak door but she hesitated, seeming to think better of it. Finally, she struck the wood and turned her attention down the neighborhood street as if looking for an escape. I was beginning to think no one was home when the door opened.

"Hello, Charlie," I heard her say.

His mouth fell open and his pale face registered shock.

"Willie—" He looked her over as if she was some sort of specter.

I got out and stood by the car figuring my sister might need me to referee.

She stared into Charlie's face. "Did you miss me?"

He found his tongue and said, "When did you get out of the slammer?"

"This morning." She smoothed her dress over her hips. "Haven't even had time to pull myself together."

A boyish grin cracked his chiseled jaw. "You look mighty together to me."

Willie looked past him into the dim house. "You going to ask me in or what?"

Charlie tore his eyes from her and jerked his head behind him.

"Uh, well—"

A hard-looking brunette wearing a silky robe came up behind Charlie.

"Who's our company, Sugar?" she said, her voice smoky.

I saw Charlie quaver.

"Willie," he said. "Willie, it's not—"

"Willie Carter?" the woman broke in. "The bootleg driver? Heard about you." She stuck her hand under Charlie's arm as if to shake with Willie.

"Sugar, is it?" Willie this time.

I saw trouble coming and stepped toward Willie.

"Things changed while you were—away," Charlie said.

When Willie spoke next, the words came with venom.

"I guess change is why you didn't come to see me."

"I meant to, Willie. I did—"

"But I kept him too busy." The woman rubbed Charlie's arm.

Willie raised her fist. "You son of a—"

I caught her wrist before the punch landed on its intended mark.

"Let's go." I tried to turn her, but she held her ground like a rhino setting up for a charge.

"Wait a minute," she said and jerked her arm away. Her eyes fastened on Charlie. "If you're still in the business, I'm looking to get back on my feet."

"You mean driving again?"

"He's finished with all that, aren't cha, Sugar?" the woman said.

Charlie's lids shut and when he opened them again, something on the stoop had him mesmerized.

"Well, ain't I the fool." Willie swiveled and marched toward the car, but over her shoulder she said, "Let's get outta here, Jimmy."

"Hey, Coochie!" Charlie called out. Willie and I both turned to see a dog burst out the door between Charlie and his new wife. Coochie, as he had called the dog, dashed to Willie and jumped up, paws at her waist.

"Girl," Willie said, "I guess you remember me, don't you?"

"This is your dog?" I asked.

"Was mine, yeah," Willie said.

Charlie stepped onto the stoop and called the dog. Coochie ignored him.

"Seems like she's your dog again," I said.

"I don't have a place for her." Willie's eyes pleaded with mine, hers wet. She'd lost Charlie and Coochie once, and now she was about to lose them both again. Seems like she'd lost about everything.

"Well—I can take her for now. I don't think Dottie will object and the boys will be thrilled." I looked back at Charlie. "If you don't think he'd mind."

"All he needs to mind is his own business," Willie said. "Let's go, Coochie."

"Willie!" Charlie called after her. "Come on, Willie!"

The woman put her arm around Charlie's neck. "Let them go, Sugar," she said.

We put Coochie in the back and she settled in, keeping her attention on Willie.

"What are you going to do, sister?" I asked when we were down the road.

"Wish I knew." She stared out the passenger window at the green lawn of Elmwood Park. Beyond the park, Rockledge Inn sat high on Mill Mountain.

"You ever been up there?" I asked.

"Took the rail tram up once. There's spectacular views of the valley for anyone who can afford a room." Her voice had sadness in it. For the last year, her view had been through iron bars.

"The tram closed last year," I said. "The crash sucked the wind out of tourist money. Even the view of the city and the Blue Ridge wasn't enough to get people to open their purses."

Willie was quiet for half a minute as we drove around a curve in the road. Then she said, "Life is fickle, isn't it?"

"I could ask about a job for you at the sawmill if you'd like," I said.

"Sawmill?" She rolled her eyes at me. "A woodcutter, Jimmy?" She shuddered.

"Seems good enough for me." I shrugged, knowing where she intended to go—to the thing she knew best—the only thing she knew.

I stopped at a rooming house that had a vacancy sign and dropped her off. Before she walked away, she reached in and ruffled Coochie's fur.

"You'll take good care of her, won't you?" she said.

"Of course I will."

"I'll see you again soon, Coochie." She kissed the dog's forehead, wiped her cheek, and turned away.

20.
Willie—1930

It was late when Jimmy dropped me off at the Blackwater Filling Station a week later. Before I got out, I said, "You mosey along now."

"Willie," he started, but I interrupted.

"No sermons, Jimmy. I know what I'm doing."

"I used to believe that. Now I'm not so sure." He gripped the wheel with both hands.

I looked toward the business of the filling station where in the darkness shadows of men were defying the law for the sake of their livelihood.

I laid my hand on Jimmy's arm. "You live your life your way." I jerked my head toward the bootleggers. "I've got to live mine my own way." I squeezed his shoulder. "Go on now, brother."

When Jimmy rolled away, I rubbed my hands together wishing I had a pair of gloves. The night was chilly for early October and the leaves were changing up on North Mountain. It was too dark to see any color, though, and if I planned to drive all night, I might as well be a bat for all the red and gold I'd see. I thought that a damned pity.

Thomas Rakes, a renowned moonshiner mean as a cottonmouth, was standing by a truck watching a dark-skinned man load barrels into the bed. Three other fellows were packing a couple other vehicles with gallon jugs. There was going to be a run tonight, and I had my sights set on being part of it.

When he saw me, Peg Hatcher elbowed Roosevelt Smith.

"Hey Roose, look what the cat dragged in." Hatcher was a good-looking fellow nearing forty and clean-shaven. He wore a tie loosely knotted at his neck and a fedora set at a saucy tilt atop his head. His ears stuck out instead of hugging his head, which gave him the look of a likable scamp.

"Well, well," Smith said. "And fresh out of the pokey."

"Fresh is the word, all right—fresh as a daisy and ready for business." I squinted through the sole streetlight to watch the vehicles being loaded. "Either of you two gentlemen need a driver?"

Hatcher rubbed his chin. "Rakes might." He tossed his chin toward the other man. "Hey Tom—who's driving tonight?"

Wisdom said to steer clear of Rakes, but I needed money, and Rakes had plenty of dough.

He slapped the black man on the shoulder. "Only got one load and Chris here knows the drill."

Roose Smith planted his fists on his narrow hips. "It wouldn't hurt to have a pilot. What do you think, Peg?"

"A pilot, huh?" Hatcher turned to me. "You remember how to drive, girl?"

"Drive? Hell, Peg, I'll sprout wings and fly."

I liked Peg Hatcher. James Walter Hatcher was his given name, but he had broken his leg as a teenager—falling off the roof of his house after imbibing some of his pa's liquor, as word had it—and the bones weren't set right. Ever since, he walked with a limp, which earned him the name Peg. He kept a fiddle in his car and sometimes while he waited for his drivers to return to the station he'd pull it out and play some tunes to keep up courage on the darkest nights.

Hatcher nodded. "Then let's get to it. We're delivering to Washington. Them senators got a big thirst."

I didn't ask about payment. At this point, I'd take anything I could get—at least until I proved myself to my new employers.

"You'll be in the Ford," Smith said. It was a newer model than Charlie's and without the protective metal welded to it. Getting shot at was a chance I'd have to take.

"Just be sure Chris is clear through to Charlottesville. He should be all right from there," Smith said.

It was two hours to Charlottesville, but I'd lead Chris on to Culpepper to be sure he was safe. I couldn't take chances with the law this time. No way I wanted to get sent up again.

"Ewell Stuart still around?" I asked. Stuart had a habit of sending drivers up the river so it looked like he was doing his elected job for the state.

"Sure is," Hatcher said. "Jo Shively's got him in the station playing poker with Sam White."

"And drinking up some of Jo's illegal liquor, no doubt," I mused.

"You didn't hear it from me," Hatcher said.

I nodded toward Chris, a dapper fellow wearing a sweater vest over a starched button-up shirt.

"You ready?" I said.

"Sure," he said. "Let's get this hooch to those lawmakers."

I gave him the high sign and climbed into the Ford.

"You sit tight. Give me twenty minutes to get ahead of you."

I screeched onto the road and fell easily into the rhythm of the gears, the growl of the engine, the wind in my ears. It was good to drive again, to press on the gas and have the machine answer. I was master of the team of horses under the hood, lashing them to sprint, their hooves holding the road around mountain curves.

Eighty. Ninety. One-ten on the straightaway.

Ahead I saw flashing lights and something across the road. My foot slammed the brake and the rear end crab-walked before the car skidded to a stop.

Four men in uniform stood by a police cruiser. Lewis Bridges approached the car window.

"Haven't seen you in a while, Willie." He pulled a cigarette from his chest pocket, lit it. "Up to your old tricks?"

"Hello Lewis." I thought back to the jail cells ringing with the song "O! Bud," and seeing Bridges brought the lyrics back to me. "Uncle Bud he died and he went to hell. He grabbed Tom Devil and he fucked him well." I had no inclination to fuck Lewis Bridges, but I sure didn't want to be locked up in that hell of the women's prison again.

Bridges blew smoke toward me. Tobacco aroma mixed with Beechnut chewing gum. Not offensive except it was the law chewing and smoking.

"You still deputy sheriff, or have you become respectable?" I said. Bridges was more an annoyance than a threat.

"I could book you right now for aiding in a crime against the government," he said.

"I'm not carrying and you know it."

Bridges raised his eyebrows and leaned in, palms on the window casing. "I know most likely you don't want to end up behind bars."

I sighed and pulled a ten-spot from my pocket.

"No, Your Honor, I don't."

Bridges took the money, folded it corner to corner and pushed it into his shirt pocket.

"That's a good girl," he said.

I lifted my nose. "How long you fellows plan to hang out here tonight?"

"We'll be clear of here within the hour." He looked over the Ford's hood. "Right, boys?"

The two other coppers nodded.

"I'll hold you to that," I said.

I slowed down until I saw the headlamps of Chris's truck behind me and congratulated myself on the ten-spot performing its duty. Maybe I was seeing things, but beyond Chris another set of headlights appeared on the road, lights flashing. The cruiser drove up alongside him and gave him the signal to pull over. Loaded with jugs, there was no way his buggy could outrun the law. I whirled the Ford around and backtracked.

When I reached the holdup, Chris had been hauled out of the car and his wrists cuffed behind him. I ground my teeth. Rakes had depended on me to see Chris through. Betrayal bit like a rabid coon and fury burned my lungs.

"Lewis, you said the road was clear," I spat.

Bridges pointed at me with his sharp chin. "And it was. Did you see any roadblock?"

"You gave your word." In my world, a man's word was sacrosanct.

"I gave my word to uphold the law," Bridges said. "What I'm doing is preventing the distribution of illegal substances."

"What you're doing is bullroar and you know it." Men like Chris had families to feed and without upstanding jobs to be had, delivering a high-demand product meant survival. And the way I saw it, undermining survival — mine as well as my partner driver's — was criminal.

"Willie Carter Sharpe, I'm placing you under arrest," Bridges said.

He had to be kidding. "For what, Lewis? You've got nothing on me."

"For disrespecting an officer." He grabbed my arm and slapped a handcuff on me. "Maybe we can get you your old jail cell." He winked at me. "Make you feel right at home."

• • •

I rolled and tumbled that night. It was bad enough being locked up again, but Chris had counted on me and I had let him down. Of course, there was no reasoning with Bridges. He was like a wolf on the prowl, and it didn't matter what kind of meat he chased so long as he caught it in his bloodthirsty fangs. He didn't have much on me, and I figured he'd let me go with a slap on the wrist. But the man in the other cell had been hauling the illegal goods and had skin the wrong color to boot. Chris was sure to be in hot water.

I couldn't reach the high window, but I watched the cell lighten as the sun rose. The guard would have to open the door to bring something to eat, and I imagined breaking past him and making a run for it. Fat chance, and I knew it. For now, there was nothing to do but watch bits of dust dance on the sunbeam.

It must have been getting on to noon when I heard voices. Unmistakably one belonged to Peg Hatcher and the other was Lewis Bridges. Papers rustled.

"Is this cashier's check bail money, Peg?" Bridges asked.

"You know it is, Lewis," Hatcher said. "Now you set those two scallywags free."

"I believe you owe me ten dollars, Sheriff," I said when I came through the office.

"Watch yourself, Willie," Bridges said. "You're only out on the good graces of Mr. Hatcher here."

I muttered "bastard" under my breath and pushed the door open, Chris following behind.

"Thanks for putting up bail, Peg," I said.

He shrugged. "Goes with the territory."

I shook my head. "If I never spend another night behind bars, it'll be too soon."

"Amen to that," Chris said.

"As long as the law is more crooked than the bootleggers," Hatcher said, "we'll be able to buy our way out of a tight spot." He twisted his head toward the two of us. "Come on, Chris— I'll buy you and Willie some breakfast."

• • •

Peg Hatcher bailed me out several more times—I've lost count how many. Bridges said he reckoned he'd have to start charging me rent on that cell but I didn't think it was a laughing matter. I changed my route to roads where I was more likely to avoid barriers and evade the law.

During the mild wet winter, I slowed down enough for the Ford's tires to grab the mud but kept up enough speed to gun through puddles. I hoped the truck Chris was driving wasn't so heavy it would get stuck in the muck. I was earning good money and had managed to avoid Charlie Sharpe, if he was still delivering liquor. Sure, I missed him, but driving required my full attention. Focusing on shifting through the gears of the fast vehicle under me took my thoughts off the hole in my heart. No man—not even Charlie—was worth a distraction.

Even in the winter, if the roads were dry on a clear night, I could make good time. When I crossed into Rockbridge County, in the moonlight I made out Natural Bridge on my left. Pop and May took Jimmy and me there once on a picnic and told us about how hundreds of millions years ago Cedar Creek had carved out a limestone mountain to make the bridge. For me, driving was like that—like brook water rushing over rocks, taking the path of least resistance, the fastest route to wherever the water was going. Natural Bridge was a sacred site for the Monacan Indians, May had said. Although I hadn't thought much about religion, I believed some spirit watched over me. An ancestor probably. Aunt Emma had died while I was in the women's prison, and I could almost see her reaching her fat arms down from heaven to protect me. May, too, hovered over me, maybe not approving of my path but loving me all the same.

Peg Hatcher told me I was the best pilot in the business but in the business of bootleg liquor, a driver could not afford to get smug. Some towns in Southwest Virginia were set on a fault that cracked the earth's surface and heaved up jagged rocks. My fault was believing I was untouchable, that the law wouldn't catch me and lock me up again.

One chilly night, the Ford's headlamps caught an obstacle across the road. Sawhorses and one cruiser. Usually a car carried two officers, but as I slowed, I saw only a single man in uniform, a man I didn't recognize. The badge on his chest glinted in the light. When I stopped, he knocked on the passenger window, which was unusual. The routine was to approach the driver's side. I leaned over and rolled down the glass.

"Awfully late to be out on the road alone, isn't it?" He had a broad mustache, not curled at the ends like a handlebar. More like a wooly bear caterpillar.

"You must be new on the force. Don't you know there's no law against driving at night?"

Standing by the blockade he couldn't know how fast I had been going. Eighty at least, I figured.

"No law unless your name is Willie Carter Sharpe."

I wasn't surprised he'd heard of me. Among police, a woman with multiple arrests for hard driving got tongues wagging.

I offered the man my hand. "Don't believe I've had the pleasure, officer."

"Deputy Sheriff Richards," he said, pressing his palm to mine. His hands were warm for such a cold night.

"I'm not carrying, Sheriff Richards."

He was looking at my jacket, leather like one that flyer Amelia Earhart wore. It cost a pretty penny, too.

"Piloting's the same as carrying. You ought to know that, Mrs. Sharpe." His breath smelled of coffee and cigarettes, either of which I would have welcomed at that moment.

His eyes rolled down to my lap. I would not go back to jail—not tonight. My jacket pocket held five ten-spots, but I'd have to move slowly in case he suspected a weapon. The air behind him was fresh and cold, piney and wormy. I'd been inhaling gas fumes for the last few hours and was almost relieved to be stopped. A ten should open the road for Chris and we'd be on our way. If he saw the Ford stopped at the barrier, he'd pull over until I conducted business with the law.

"Look—can't we settle this in a friendly manner?" I gripped the wheel and forced my face into a pleasant expression. "I've got something that might—"

"Turn off the engine," Richards interrupted. He opened the door and slid in beside me before I could reach for the money.

"How friendly are you prepared to be?" He unbuckled the belt diagonal across his chest as if to say he was off duty. He might have smiled but I couldn't be sure under the wooly bear.

Anything to stay out of the clink, I thought as he opened his coat and unbuttoned his pants. Then he looked at me and tilted his head toward his crotch.

"So that's the game," I said.

Anything.

I turned toward him and reached through the trousers to find him flaccid, easy to pull through the opening.

Anything.

I spit on my palm and massaged the organ until I felt it stiffen. Richards reached behind my head and pulled me down.

Anything.

My hip pressed hard against the wheel and pain shot down my leg.

He was strong, his sex filling my mouth, strangling me. I struggled to draw a breath. My lungs burned and I willed myself not to gag as he found the back of my throat. My lips covered my teeth. If I bit him, I'd no doubt rot in jail for the rest of my life.

Anything.

His breathing came quicker, his round stomach bulging against my ear. Finally, he cried out, a cry of pain and release and ecstasy, and my mouth filled with so much gluey substance that again I nearly suffocated.

He released my head and I opened my door and spat on the road. Coughed and spat again. When I sat up and wiped my mouth, Richards was still beside me. He had drawn a wad of bills from a pocket. It looked to be hundreds of dollars. He separated a few bills and handed them to me.

"Where'd you get that kind of money?" I tried to hide my surprise, the ridiculousness of me intending to pay him and have the tables turned.

"Still operators have to pay some hefty fines." He winked — actually winked at me. "Expect I'll see you again, Mrs. Sharpe."

He pulled himself together, got out, and moved the sawhorse. When I started the car and drove slowly by him, I heard him say, "You all drive safely, now."

I shook my head. "I'll be damned," I said and gunned the engine.

. . .

Whenever I scouted the route, Richards was on patrol at the roadblock waiting for me. My reward for front-seat services always cleared the road for deliveries and earned me a few more greenbacks. Richards and I got to be good friends. Not lovers, exactly, because the loving went only one way. Jeff, as he told me to call him, short for Jefferson, was married but figured as long as we kept our business sitting up instead of lying down, he wasn't cheating. Married or not, a man wanted an outlet. Some men, if they needed relief, looked at magazines behind the closed door of the bathroom. Others, like Jeff Richards, had a desire for a little help with his fantasies. In our partnership, we both got what we wanted.

For weeks I piloted trucks loaded with moonshine, careening around curves and kicking up dust on straightaways, stopping for a few scandalous minutes with Richards. We got along so well he gave me a raise—twenty-five bucks at a go. Hatcher and Roose also handed me fistfuls of money which I spent before it cooled from their hot hands. I bought myself a Buick touring car, furs, and a collection of shoes that would make the Queen of England envious. I became two people, the respectable woman of daylight whom shop girls welcomed with courtesy and admiration, and the working woman of the night skilled in the business of delivering bootleg liquor to thirsty customers and pleasure to men barring the way. If I got myself into trouble, Hatcher was always there to settle a simple misdemeanor charge and get me on the road again.

21.
Jimmy — 1931

Bootleggers knew their way around the law. In fact, I came to understand law officers were some of their best customers. A healthy share of the take, and they turned a blind eye — often an intoxicated one. What was the harm?

The harm, it soon became clear, was from the aforementioned federal officer named Sam White. Newspapers reported that Willie had a reward of fifty government dollars on her head, and I figured White aimed to get that money. He was still rankled about her pilot car ramming the cruiser and breaking his arm when she was working with Charlie Sharpe.

Hatcher had recommended Willie lie low someplace out of Virginia's borders, someplace where White couldn't track her down. That's when she called me.

You'd have to understand my situation. Dottie and I grew up together. We were sweet on each other from the start and had our first kiss when we were twelve. One summer afternoon we met up at the Mabry Mill on Robertson's Creek with the sun beating down hot enough to raise a blister and the air like a Chinese laundry. Dottie was having a picnic with her parents, and I suggested we take a dip in the river to cool off. She picked up a tick hiking through bushes to the water, and the head was dug in her thigh. Dottie hated ticks, and I offered to get it out, head and all. You had to get out the head or else you might get Rocky Mountain Spotted Fever, so I pinched deep enough to make her squeal, but I had to be sure I got the whole eight-legged beast. Ticks don't have brains except for sensors in their guts. Their heads are used only for eating. They find you by the warmth of your skin, and later I found out Dottie was plenty warm. Oh boy, was she! Anyway, I got the tick and squashed it between two rocks. Dottie was so happy she hugged me, and before I knew it we were kissing. I'd never kissed a girl before but I sure liked it, and by the way Dottie kissed me, I could tell she did, too. Unfortunately, her pa came looking for her before we got very far, but I was already charmed.

When we were thirteen she let me put my hand up her shirt and feel her breasts, what there was of them. I reckoned breasts were like cow udders since both produce milk for their young, but Dottie's were just forming and soft as a newborn piglet except for the marble-hard center. She said the nipples got hard when she was cold or excited. I was getting pretty excited myself touching her there. It was different from being with Lila. Where Lila had my body, Dottie had my heart.

One thing led to another, as you might imagine, and Dottie and I found more time to spend together away from prying eyes. The first time she touched me below the belt was a disaster, and I had to sneak into the house without May seeing the wet splotch on my dungarees. After that, I learned to control my impulses by thinking about baseball. The Cincinnati Reds had the fewest strikeouts that season, and Babe Ruth broke the homerun record for the third season in a row. But there was Dottie with her hands on me and mine under her skirt and by the time we were in our last year of school, her father was coming to visit my father with a shotgun. It wasn't entirely my fault. It was the perfume of her skin — what soap had she used to wash? The warmth of blood under the crook of her elbow, the velvet of her thigh, my delirious abandonment of all reason when her hand made soft strokes on me as if she was petting a puppy so I nearly burst through my blue jeans.

I'd probably have married her anyway, but we jumpstarted things a bit. Anyway, boy number two followed on his brother's heels. Dottie put on some weight and was not as eager to cozy up to me in bed as she used to be, but Pop said that was the way marriage operated. I went to see him as much as I could after May died. Usually I'd bring him one of Dottie's covered dishes because he lived on canned soup otherwise. But he kept working, saying it got him in better shape than those rich fellows going to a gym to exercise.

Things got rough between Dottie and me when Willie asked me to drive with her out west. Willie was like May, trying to elevate her social status with nice clothes and that diamond chip she had in her teeth. For the life of me, I don't know where she got that idea. It seemed low-class to me, even though the diamond must have cost her a bundle. May eventually resigned herself to life on the farm, but she always encouraged Willie to reach for the stars. My sister reached high, all right, until the ladder fell out from under her. Now she was asking me to help her back up.

Dottie wasn't keen on me taking a leave from work, what with two kids for her to keep up with. Willie said a family would be good cover for her and they ought to come along, but Dottie dug in her heels. Our little ones were in school and without a clue about where Willie was taking me, it didn't make sense. Besides, Dottie said, my sister was a criminal and she didn't want her children associating with a fugitive. But Willie and I were blood, so I didn't have much choice but to help her out.

When she called, I told her we should take the train.

"Too public," she said, her voice crackling over the line. "We'll take the Buick."

"Don't you think you'd be recognized driving that rig?"

"If they want me, they'll have to catch me," she said. "I'll pick you up in an hour."

I kissed my wife and kids and said I'd be back as soon as I helped Willie get settled somewhere. "Give me a week—that's a promise."

Coochie pushed her nose against my knee. She must have sensed the trip had something to do with Willie.

"Can't take you, Cooch. Sorry. I'm not sure where we're going myself."

"You're aiding and abetting," Dottie said.

"I'm helping my sister," I answered.

"You'll end up in a cell with her, and then what will we do?"

"A week," I said. "My word."

•   •   •

The top was up on the Buick, a soft yellow color. Willie wore a blouse Dottie would have called chiffon and a calf-length skirt flared at the bottom to give her legs room for working the pedals in her high heel shoes with straps that crossed over her foot. She must have paid twenty dollars for the outfit. A fur coat was slung across the back seat and at first I thought it was a dead animal. Style was everything when Willie was off duty.

She was pretty eager to get out of Virginia and gripped the wheel so tight I could see muscles rippling under her skin.

"Do you know where we're heading?" I asked.

"Toward the Mississippi River."

"Louisville?"

"The feds might be expecting me in Louisville. We'll stop there but it's a better bet to go farther west."

"Louisville is close to ten hours, Willie," I said. "I'll have to drive some of the way to give you a rest."

"I can make it in six."

"We'll see about that," I said.

"Once we get over the Appalachians, it's all flat. Should be able to wind out the six cylinders to a hundred." Already we were outside the city and nearly to Christiansburg. "I've delivered to Louisville lots of times," she said. "You hold on tight, Jimmy, and stop worrying."

"You have a plan for when we reach Louisville?"

She nodded, all business. I'd never seen her so focused. This must have been how she was when she piloted.

"Peg's arranged for some—" She hesitated to find the right word. "Some associates to take care of us there—on the Q.T."

I had to trust Willie, just as I'd trusted her when I was a kid. The question was—could I trust Peg Hatcher?

Willie handed me a jar of clear liquid, and I was glad to taste water and not moonshine. We needed our wits about us. She had a bag of sandwiches, and Dottie had wrapped up some cookies and an apple each for us. We'd have to make a couple stops for gasoline and washroom breaks, but otherwise we were kicking up dust on lonesome country roads.

Once we got through the mountain passes, I allowed a deep breath. Willie seemed relieved, too, and on the straightaway she slowed the Buick to sixty. Night had fallen and I could see nothing but flat fields on either side of us. No sawhorse barriers, no flashing lights. Stars hung low in the black sky like sparks hovering over us.

"You okay?" I asked Willie.

She shrugged. "Life—it's nothing but a delivery from one place to another." She flashed her eyes at me. "Never had you on a delivery before, little brother."

"We're like that fellow Huckleberry from the book," I said. "Did you read it?"

"I believe I read that one during those prison years we were forced to sit with books. That's the one about the kid on the raft with the runaway slave, isn't it?"

"I guess we're sort of like Huck and his friend—Jim, I think his name was. Floating down the river in a big yellow Buick." I laughed at my own joke.

"And being chased," Willie said. "But by feds instead of slave hunters."

"Jim was wanted because of the color of his skin. You're being chased for duping the government out of its tax money."

"That liquor comes from farmers' fields, Jimmy. It's all natural, made on their own property. There shouldn't be a law against it."

"There's no law against making it and drinking it. The law is against selling it."

"Then, that's the hot pickle, isn't it? Can't argue with supply and demand." She considered for a few seconds. "You know, bootleg drivers are like roaches, Jimmy. We come out at night and profit on the prosperity of our hosts. Roaches have been around for thousands of years. Bombs could destroy most of humanity and there'll still be roaches. And there will always be moonshine, too. Difference is, most of us would rather have a drink than deal with bugs."

"That is a pickle for sure," I said.

A quiet settled between us until I asked, "Does this business make you happy, Willie?" I meant illegal driving, but we both understood that her work required dodging the law.

"Are *you* happy, little brother?" she countered.

"I guess so." I hadn't paused long enough to consider happiness. I had a job, a family, a roof over my head, food on the table. What more was there? But happy? I don't remember being happy except for whittling a piece of wood. But that was more than a decade ago when I hadn't a care.

"I'm not convinced grown men are supposed to be happy," I said.

"I try not to think about myself," she said, "except for getting dressed and putting grub down my craw. Other than that, I manage."

I looked through the windshield at the road lighted by the car's headlamps. "Is this what you call managing?"

Willie didn't answer right away. After a few breaths she said, "I wouldn't call it despair. Or even sadness. I've got a pillowcase full of cash, and driving makes my heart beat faster. Maybe that's happiness."

"But afterward you go to your room alone?"

She sighed. "It's all ebb and flow. Everything is ebb and flow, Jimmy."

"I suppose getting thrown in jail is the ebb." I was walking on the edge of a volcano, but I knew Willie well enough that she wouldn't erupt—at least not with me.

"You know they won't even allow you to bring your own pajamas? It's as if they want to take your name away—your very self. They want you to feel like you're nothing."

"We make our own luck, Willie. May used to call it destiny. She made hers when she married Pop. You can make yours if you go straight."

"Too late for that," she said. "There's no solid ground under my feet."

It was near midnight and we were in Kentucky, closing in on Lexington when I started feeling drowsy. Willie was saying something about good days and bad days and how the dark valley between the good days seemed to stretch to eternity. How sometimes she loses her bearings, and I knew she wasn't talking about navigating country roads at night. She meant figuring out what she was doing with her life. And she meant loneliness, no one to sort out her thoughts with. I'd never thought of Willie being lonely or of having demons, I guess you could say. Or maybe I was too comfortable. Maybe comfort is a demon, too.

I must have fallen asleep for a few hours because a ghost of light behind us told me it was early morning.

"You're sure a lot of company, little brother," Willie said, sarcastic-like.

I rubbed my eyes. "Are we near Louisville?"

"Passed it," she said.

"I thought we were stopping—"

"Peg's men waved us on," she snapped. "Agents everywhere. Seems they all want a piece of that fifty." Her face was blanched. She'd been driving for nearly twelve hours.

"Aren't you bushed?" I said. "I could take over for a while and let you rest."

"I'm fine, Junebug." When she used my childhood name, I knew she was about to crack.

"Sure, Willie." Suddenly I was an eleven-year-old boy again, bending to my older sister's authority.

"Listen," she said. "I live like a mole, underground, out of sight. Daylight is my enemy. I'm like one of those nocturnal animals—a badger or a coon."

"Or a porcupine?"

She didn't laugh when I tried to lighten the mood. "I'm not the one with the quills. That's Sam White. And he'll stick them in me if he gets a chance."

A minute went by before I asked, "Where are you thinking of stopping?"

"Saint Louis. White won't go that far even for the piddling reward."

"How far are we from Saint Louis?"

"Two hours." Her voice was softer. "Peg's friend at the station said the coast would be clear there." She leaned her head from side to side, stretching her neck. "I can make it."

•　•　•

In Saint Louis I saw to it Willie was set up in a boarding house on McPherson Avenue. She used the name Wilhelmina Collins to throw off the law. The rooming house had a garage where she kept the Buick.

"You might have to sell the car," I told her. "It's a dead giveaway."

"Break my heart, why don't you, Jimmy," she said. "And I suppose you want me to have this gem removed from my tooth?"

"Might not be a bad idea either."

"What kind of a brother are you?"

"One that wants to keep you out of the clink, sister," I said.

When she was settled in, I hugged her goodbye and caught a Twin Coach bus to Roanoke. That was the last I saw of Willie until I visited her at the Alderson Reformatory near Lewisburg, West Virginia.

22.
Willie — 1933

Old Sam White had his nose to the ground, bloodhound that he was. He picked up my scent within a week. Either he was hard up for cash and needed half a C-note or he was determined to wreak vengeance. Maybe both.

He gave me a free ride east, anyway. Alderson was one of the cushiest women's prisons in the country. I had a bunkmate to talk to, and there were arts and crafts classes and even a volleyball team. I couldn't picture myself playing volleyball, but it might have done me some good.

Some of the women kept up with the latest news, and we even had radio privileges after supper. New York's governor, a fellow named Roosevelt, had been elected U.S. President over Hoover in a landslide victory. I'd rather say the depression, mass unemployment, and Prohibition defeated old Herbert, and good riddance to him. One of Roosevelt's first actions was signing a law allowing the sale of beer and wine, the first legal alcohol in nearly a decade and a half. Prohibition was the cause of the bootleg whiskey industry which the federal government claimed had cheated it out of eleven billion dollars in tax revenue. On top of that, the feds had wasted a hundred million dollars trying to catch those of us profiting from the said industry. I had to agree with the new president — it was time to move on.

Probably the law against hard liquor would be eased up next, in which case it looked like I wouldn't be needed to transport hooch again. Even though some restrictions on alcohol had been lifted, the government wanted to punish those robbing it of funds and since most illegal whiskey came from southwest Virginia, that was the reach of the long arm of the law.

The incarcerated ladies and I listened to Roosevelt's fireside chats and The Lone Ranger, a masked cowboy who fought outlaws—like me, I guess—with his Indian friend Tonto. I liked The Oldsmobile Program for the singing and comedy acts. If the producers had heard me singing to Coochie, they might have had me on the show. As it was, I sure missed that dog—even more than I missed Charlie, truth be told.

I missed home, too, even though I wasn't sure what that meant anymore. Pop's farm was home until I left without a backward glance. Now that I had time, I thought about how I used to run across the farm fields and stubbed my bare toe against a stone or felt satisfaction at a freshly plowed field, rich with possibility. How I loved the heady sweet smell of apple and pear falls rotting under trees in the orchard. In early summer when I couldn't wait for the fruit to ripen, I plucked hard treasures from the branches and gorged until they gave me a bellyache. Hundreds of times I'd sat at May's table, my mouth watering at the aroma of a kettle of her green beans—ones I'd snapped fresh from the kitchen garden—cooked most of a day with a slab of pork fat until they melted on the tongue. Or a pot of her pinto beans in their own gravy we sopped with triangles of skillet cornbread. On clear days when I hoed at the kitchen garden I stopped to watch swallows swoop over the barn in an airborne dance, all of them attuned to others in the flock. My flock now was other lawless women thrown behind bars for any number of crimes—stealing their way out of poverty, selling themselves on the streets, assault with a weapon against men who raped them or beat them or, in a few cases, tried to kill them. Most were poor—teenagers, single mothers, women of color, all of them down on their luck. If home was a dwelling place, I guessed for me, at least in the past few years, that would be behind iron bars. I had dwelt there more times than I'd have liked. For a few years Charlie's place had felt like home, but I'd given that up. No point in looking at what was never meant to be. If I admitted it, my most comfortable dwelling place was in a fast car, my fingers wrapped around a steering wheel, shifting through fifteen gears and doing eighty on mountain roads. I didn't think I'd ever feel like I belonged anyplace else.

I lost track of time—how long had I been locked up at Alderson? Months, I reckoned. Then one day the guard came to get me between breakfast and lunch.

"You have a visitor, Mrs. Sharpe," he said.

My thoughts went right to Charlie, but if he was coming to apologize to me, I didn't want to see him. I blamed him for the situation I was in, and an apology was not going to change anything. Then I thought, Jimmy, and my heart felt lighter. My brother always raised my spirits, and maybe he'd have good news for me. An appeal or probation or Sam White had come to his senses and dropped the charges.

The guard unlocked the bars and led me to a small room with no window and nothing but a desk with a chair on either side of it. He motioned me to the seat facing the door.

"Who is it?" I asked.

"A gentleman," was all he said.

There was a clock on the wall, and I watched the minutes tick by. If the visitor was here, what was taking so long? Were they checking his pockets for files and weapons? Five minutes went by—then eight, then ten.

Thinking the fellow had changed his mind, I was about to ask the guard to take me back to my cell when the door opened and in walked a man in a gray suit, tie, short hair slicked down, a little paunchy and a dead-serious look about him. Probably in his forties. He'd come to do some business and he was all business about it.

"Good morning, Mrs. Sharpe," he said. "My name is Frank Tavenner. I'm an attorney for the Western District of Virginia." He offered his hand to me and I took it. But what would an attorney want with me? Had Jimmy hired him to help me?

"I hope you plan to get me out of here, Mr. Tavenner." I looked up at him. He was taller than the guard and held himself straight. No slouch to him.

The guard watched for a minute to be sure I wasn't going to attack the lawyer. Then Tavenner nodded to him and the guard backed out and closed the door. Tavenner pulled out the empty chair and sat opposite me. He settled himself on the hard wood and swung a leather briefcase up and onto the table between us. He smelled of aftershave or hair tonic—I couldn't tell which. Clean-shaven, he wore a neatly pressed suit and reminded me of John Carter—except not so good-looking and on the other side of the law.

He pushed the briefcase aside, wove his fingers together in front of him, and placed them on the table as if to show he wasn't carrying a gun. "Do you know why you're in Alderson, Mrs. Sharpe?"

I met his eyes. "I have a suspicion."

He didn't laugh but opened the briefcase and slid out some papers.

"They've got you on reckless driving and conspiring to cheat the United States government out of tax revenue by selling liquor."

I opened my hands to show I had nothing to hide. "I wasn't cheating anybody and I wasn't selling anything. Since when did driving become a crime?"

Tavenner's eyes were green. He blinked at the overhead light before he spoke. "In any event, those are serious charges that could keep you incarcerated for a very long time."

"If somebody hired you to be my lawyer, I'm hoping you've got better news for me."

"I might have some good news," Tavenner said, "but it comes at a price."

"For good news, I can get my hands on money, if that's what you're asking." Money wasn't a problem so long as Peg Hatcher had my back. But, then, Peg might have been in the same bind I was in and be looking for somebody to bail him out.

"It's not about money, Mrs. Sharpe." He tapped an index finger on the wood tabletop. "You probably know that Sheriff Hodges divided Franklin county into districts and assigned deputies to oversee operation of stills. Part of their job was to collect protection money—twenty-five dollars per still and ten dollars per load of whiskey."

"I'm not privy to all those details," I said.

"Then you may not know that Ewell Stuart has been indicted for being a ringleader of the conspiracy."

"I'd heard rumblings along those lines, yes." I crossed my arms over my chest. "It's about time they got that scoundrel."

"He's not the only one," the attorney said. "It seems there were dozens of hands in the pot, including yours."

I tilted my head and gave him the side-eye. "So where's the good news?"

Tavenner allowed a quick half smile. "Judge Paul will be presiding over the trial. We've spoken, and he agrees to absolve you of all charges."

"Absolve me?" I wanted to be sure I understood.

"The charges would be dropped. You'd be free to leave Alderson."

"Is this a trick?" I knew better than to trust any lawman, especially not a judge.

"Not a trick, no," Tavenner said. "But there are two conditions."

Conditions. I should have guessed that would be the case. I scanned the room and then looked at the lawyer. From the expression on his face, he wasn't asking for sexual favors. But I'd do about anything to get out. Desperation was not how I had planned to live my life, but yes, I was desperate. When I got into the bootleg business, customers were happy to see me, thanked me, even told me to drive carefully. I got more kick out of driving darefully. But there was no kick rotting in a jail cell.

"I'm listening," I said.

"The first condition is that you agree to be a witness for the prosecution."

"The prosecution? You mean I'd be a stoolpigeon?"

"I wouldn't use that word," he said. "But you will be called to testify in court."

He meant testify against Peg Hatcher, Roose, even Charlie Sharpe. Peg had been good to me, but Charlie had broken faith with me. As for Ewell Stuart, I wouldn't mind taking him down.

I lifted my eyebrows. "That's it? Just tell the truth?"

"The truth as far as you know it, yes." Tavenner sat up straighter and skimmed the paper in front of him. "The other condition is that you never involve yourself with any aspect of moving liquor again. You'll have to stay clean as a whistle. If you get caught in any illegal activity, you could end up spending the rest of your life in a jail cell."

"They'd never catch me," I said. "It was just bad luck I landed in this joint."

Tavenner paused a few seconds to study my face. "Do you mind if I ask how old you are, Mrs. Sharpe?"

I snorted. "Turned thirty last week. The guards should've handed out party hats and ice cream."

From his inside coat pocket he produced a pen and wrote something on the paper.

"Thirty. And you've been incarcerated—" He ran a finger down the page. "You've been jailed thirteen times, Mrs. Sharpe. Chances are good you'd be caught again."

I planted my forearm on the table and leaned forward. "You know if I sell out, someone's likely to come after me. Can't the government offer me some protection?"

Tavenner gave a slight wag of his head and sucked his teeth.

"Afraid not. You'll have to decide if you want to take the risk."

"I'll be on the run again. But this time it'll be from the men I worked for trying to get even." Sending me behind bars again wouldn't be good enough. I'd been lucky dodging bullets before, but this time they'd put me in front of a firing squad, and no welded metal would protect me.

I watched Tavenner take a breath. His face was empty of expression. He might get me out of prison, but he'd be no help to me after that. No one would help me.

Finally the attorney said, "I'm asking you to testify about your activities with bootleggers and county officials. And I'm asking you to stay clean."

"Stay clean? How am I supposed to live? Driving's all I know." I would not cry. Willie Carter Sharpe did not cry.

"I can't offer you advice about that. All I can offer is your freedom on those two conditions."

So what was it going to be? Living inside four walls until I turn gray and bent? Arts and crafts for the next fifty years? Or being a turncoat and watching my back every minute until Stuart and White and the others forget about me?

Another minute ticked by. Tavenner wove the fingers of his hands together again and waited as if he had all day. I knew what he wanted. It was a devil's bargain.

"Who'll be asking me the questions?" I said.

"I will."

I thought Tavenner might take my hand, a fatherly gesture. But he put his palms down on the table.

"You'll have to trust me." His tone of voice had an earnestness in it. But trust an attorney, a man who was probably responsible for sending me behind bars?

I looked around the bare room. Not a window or a single picture on the cream-colored walls. If I refused his offer, this would be my life—grim and bleak. The lawyer's proposal would put me on the run. Not promising options.

"Do you want to give me an answer now, or do you need another week to think about it?" He turned his wrist and looked at his watch. He was a busy man. A successful, busy attorney who'd gotten all the right breaks.

There was a chance—a faint one—that the men I helped convict would serve their time and get on with their lives. A faint chance they'd forget about me—especially if I made sure they never laid eyes on me again. A faint chance I was willing to cling to.

"I don't need another minute in this clink, Mr. Tavenner," I said.

"I don't blame you one bit." He turned a paper around on the table and laid a pen next to it. "Sign here."

I hesitated. I hadn't expected to sign anything, especially what looked like a legal document.

"It's not a trick," Tavenner said. "It means you walk out of here a free woman."

Walk the hell where? There was nothing waiting for me. Nothing at all. Except maybe Jimmy. Jimmy the daydreamer. Jimmy who as far as I knew never broke a law or a promise.

My brother who Pop knew would never be able to run the farm. Junebug who looked up to me and believed in me. I had let him down. Of my many regrets, that was the biggest— letting Jimmy down.

As if it was a stinging nettle, carefully I picked up the pen. At the bottom of the sheet was my name — Willie Carter Sharpe. The name looked strange all of a sudden, as if I'd made it up the way I'd made up other names for myself over the years. There had been so many versions of Wilhelmina Collins that I wasn't even sure who I was anymore. Willie Carter Sharpe, the names of two men. Both had taken me down a road that led to riches and jail cells. If I had it to do over, I'd have walked away from silks and diamonds, pearls and nights of boozy arguments and made an honest woman of myself in the arms of Charlie Sharpe, the only man I'd ever loved. But there were no do-overs.

Above the name was a line for my signature. An empty line waiting for the lawyer's ink.

After I signed, Tavenner nestled the paper into his briefcase, capped the ink pen, and dropped it into his jacket pocket. Then he surveyed the small interrogation room.

"Now let's get you out of here," he said.

For the first time in our meeting, I smiled.

Tavenner frowned. "One more thing," he said. "You should think seriously about having that gem removed from your front tooth. The sparkle might cast you in a questionable light."

Then, raising his voice toward the closed door, he called for the guard.

23.
Jimmy — April 1935

After she was released from Alderson, Willie spent a year at her Saint Louis boarding house. She sold the Buick as I advised and had barely enough money to see her through. She told me without driving, she'd thought about turning tricks and decided against it. My sister may have been in the whiskey business, but she was no prostitute.

On a warm April morning, I arrived early at the Harrisonburg courthouse. The trial had been moved from Roanoke to try and avoid witness tampering. Harrisonburg in Rockingham County was over a hundred miles north of Roanoke, halfway to Washington, and the jury would be men most defendants and witnesses wouldn't know. When other Harrisonburg courthouses had burned or fallen into disrepair, the county tore them down and built the solid brick structure on Court Square it would take a mighty tornado to shake, a building that exuded dignity and demanded respect from those who entered it.

I was watchful driving into the downtown area so as not to run into a horse and buggy. Mennonites moved to the city a hundred years ago. Nobody seemed to bother them, and they minded their own business, which was farming and selling their produce in town. I supposed that was why Harrisonburg came to be known as the friendly city. Maybe their presence near Court Square would bring Willie some good luck.

Willie was to be one of 176 witnesses for the prosecution. I hoped she'd be questioned on the first day because I wouldn't be able to leave work and the family to drive so far if I had to go to the trial every day. I was proud of her, though. She had left her criminal days behind. What was next neither she nor I could tell.

At the courthouse spectators jammed the steps trying to get inside. I recognized some folks who had come from Roanoke as I did, but news of the trial to defraud the federal government of tax money had been in papers all over the country. I imagined the hotels were filled with out-of-towners.

I wedged my way through the crowd, mostly white folks but also people of color. Some dark-skinned men made liquor, too, some delivered it, and lots of them were customers who bought it. And many of them had put in their time behind bars. They were as curious as anybody else. Whiskey didn't mind who poured it down their throats so long as they paid the price.

I was almost to the door when a fellow with a bulky camera nudged my arm.

"Say—" he said. "Aren't you Willie Carter Sharpe's brother? Sure look like him. Can I get a shot of you for the evening paper?"

I jerked my arm away.

"C'mon, buddy," the reporter said, his flatcap askew over a shaggy head. "How about a word or two about your sister? What was it like growing up with her? You ever ride with her on one of her night deliveries?"

"You've got the wrong—" I started.

"James," isn't it?" the man said. "James Collins. Jimmy, she calls you. I looked you up."

Someone shoved me from behind, knocking me into a woman. "Sorry," I said to her, glad for an escape from the reporter. Making my way to the door was like riding a wild mustang. The smells of hot cement, perfume and hair tonic, musk and onion breath brought me to cough into my fist. A field of fedoras pushed forward. Mixed in, feathered hats flashed over red lipstick and red fingernails, all eager to see their neighbors from whom they no doubt had bought liquor. If the fickle hand of fortune had been pointed a different direction, they might themselves have been witnesses for one side or the other.

Every seat in the courtroom was occupied and people stood at the back, shoulder-to-shoulder, three deep. Near the front, a dozen men in suits sat around a large rectangular table. I recognized Ewell Stuart and Lewis Bridges beside two of the lawyers, both defendants dressed in expensive-looking suits, suits they may have bought with protection money they collected. Injustice went deeper than tax evasion. Injustice was taking money from struggling farmers trying to make a few bucks from their own barley and corn. May God forgive me—I hoped they both rotted in jail.

Even the room's high ceiling could not disperse the heat of bodies jammed in, and I mopped my forehead with a handkerchief. I expected a delay, but it was most of an hour before twelve white men came through a back door and side-stepped into what must have been the jury box. One of them wore a bow tie, a couple others had long ties around their collared shirts, and one was in overalls that looked to be newly laundered. They were average Joes who would pass judgment on their Franklin County neighbors, maybe even on their friends. It must have taken weeks to find men who would swear to be neutral in their decisions.

Between the jury box and the judge's desk, the witness box held a single chair facing the attorneys and spectators. It looked to me the jury members were able to see everything in the courtroom — the witness, the judge, and the attorneys, all pretty much full-face.

The clerk, I believed he was called, asked us all to stand. I was already standing, of course, and wished I'd had a seat to stand from. The man introduced Judge John Paul, who climbed a few steps to sit in a tall leather swivel chair behind the wooden desk. He must have been in his sixties, balding with round wire-rimmed glasses perched on his nose. Even behind his long black robe I could see he was paunchy, a man who had enough legal money to satisfy his appetite.

I caught sight of Willie sitting near the front. I'd have recognized her even from behind. She was dressed in white and a white rolled-brim hat to match. Lois must have helped her pick out the innocent-looking outfit. I hadn't seen my sister in white even at her wedding to Floyd Carter. But everything was at stake in this trial.

The clerk called for people to be seated, and the judge banged his wood gavel on the desktop.

"Clerk," he said to the man who wore a suit that looked a size too small for him, "you will you read the indictment." And so it began, moonshiners trying to make a living against a government trying to prevent them from earning it.

In his hands the clerk held a document that was at least twenty pages thick.

"As the names are called," he boomed so those of us in the back could hear, "each defendant please rise and state whether you plead guilty or not guilty."

I sighed. It would take a good while to read the names of at least eighty conspirators and co-conspirators and have them respond. I could've told the judge and jury they'd all plead not guilty and saved us a lot of time and trouble. Most of the men were strangers to me, but I recognized a few from the one time I hung around the filling station. Ewell Stuart, J. O. Shively,

Roosevelt Smith, Walter Hatcher, and Will Hodges. As expected, they pleaded innocent of the charge.

When finally the clerk reached the end of the list, Judge Paul said, "Each of these men has been indicted on a charge of conspiracy against the Federal government. A conspiracy is an agreement between two or more persons to do an unlawful thing or to do a lawful thing by unlawful means."

I was puzzled about how selling your own liquor could be called a conspiracy any more than setting up a lemonade stand on the side of the road. There might have been a conspiracy to kill President Lincoln, and that fellow John Brown conspired with his abolitionist partners to free the slaves before the Civil War. But the moonshiners hadn't hurt anybody. All they did was sell a little celebration drink to eager customers. Their fault, if there was one, was selling too much of it.

The judge looked at the two lawyers. "Mr. Timberlake, Mr. Tavenner, do you find any reason why these defendants should not be arraigned?"

I recognized Tavenner from Willie's description of him. The other fellow must have been Timberlake—Stephen Timberlake, I believe his name was. He was a defense attorney from Staunton, according to the papers. His slight build barely filled out a sharply pressed dark suit. Whereas Tavenner had a relaxed look about him, Timberlake's starched white shirt and perfectly knotted tie showed he was a man of precision. If anyone could get Ewell Stuart off the hook, I'd bet on Timberlake.

Timberlake stood up behind the table.

"Your honor," he said, "I move to sever the case against my client, Franklin County Commonwealth's Attorney Ewell Stuart, who is charged with accepting bribes." He held up a sheet of paper. "These allegations are separate and distinct from the other charges in the indictment. It would be severely prejudicial for Mr. Stuart to have to sit throughout the trial and listen to evidence that has no reference to him."

If I understood the meaning of prejudicial, Timberlake was accusing the judge of prejudice against Stuart. Seems to me he might be walking on dangerous ground. I wondered if he had ruffled the judge's feathers.

"Mr. Timberlake," the judge said, "Mr. Stuart will not be tried on a charge of accepting bribes, nor will the other defendants be tried on specific overt tasks, but they will all be tried for conspiracy."

You tell him, Judge Paul, I thought. But Timberlake wasn't finished.

"May it please the court, gentlemen of the jury," he said, "Ewell Stuart is a grand-nephew of a distinguished general of the Confederacy who sacrificed his life in the cause of the South, and he has a name to uphold which would not permit him to stoop to the things that the government charges." He waved his hand toward Stuart. "The evidence will bear out the innocence of Mr. Stuart, who has always comported himself with honor and integrity."

Did Timberlake mean the law didn't apply to decedents of immortal leaders? In that case, most of the other defendants were in the hot seat.

I had to respect Judge Paul, and I'd match his integrity against Stuart's anytime. He dismissed Timberlake's comment with his own. "So noted." Then he turned his attention to Tavenner.

"Mr. Tavenner, you will call your first witness."

Tavenner rose. "The prosecution calls to the stand Lewis Bridges."

The clerk made Bridges swear to tell the whole truth and nothing but it. Bridges's hair was slicked across his head, a mean look on his face, and a bow tie crooked at the neck of his shirt. He took a seat in the witness chair.

Tavenner walked toward the chair but stopped short of standing directly in front of Bridges.

"Mr. Bridges," he said, "were you at one time a deputy sheriff for Franklin County?"

"I was, from 1924 to 1930," Bridges said.

"Who was sheriff at that time?"

"That would be Pete Hodges."

Tavenner hesitated, loading ammunition into his gun, I'd guess.

"Was Sheriff Hodges an honest man, as far as you know?"

"Hodges assigned deputies to each district. We were to collect protection money from moonshiners. A granny fee is what he called it."

Protection money. Was that even legal? Was Bridges accusing the sheriff of wrongdoing?

"Do you recall meeting with Sheriff Hodges in December 1928 in Rocky Mount?" Tavenner asked.

"I was called to Sheriff Hodges's office in Rocky Mount by a letter written on Ewell Stuart's stationery and signed with Ewell Stuart's name."

"What happened at that meeting?" Tavenner strolled over to his desk as if to make a note.

"Hodges asked how many stills we had going. I told him none."

"Did Sheriff Hodges say anything further?"

"He said there was an old still in the clerk's office and they'd leave the door open. I was to get it out. A man would give me fifty dollars for the still and other equipment."

Tavenner raised his eyebrows. "What did you say?"

"I said, 'Somebody's liable to go to the penitentiary for that,' and Hodges says, 'Me and Ewell Stuart paid out two thousand dollars in our election campaign and we've got to get our money back.'" He shifted his eyes toward Stuart and then quickly again to Tavenner. "He told us to raid the stills that weren't paying. Then Stuart said, 'You catch them and we'll have them put in jail until they will be glad to pay to get out.' He said to go out and advise people to make whiskey and boost business."

Did Bridges mean the business of blackmailing moonshiners? Sheriff Hodges could spend a long time in prison himself for that crime. I was starting to see how deep the criminal activity went.

"Did you put distillers in jail?" Tavenner said.

"I did not. The following February I got a letter from Hodges asking me to resign. Hodges never would talk to me about it again."

Sounded to me like Bridges was trying to save his own behind. I saw Willie shift in her seat. She had told me the deputy was an honest man, but he had taken Willie's money to let her through a barrier more than once. Whether he had accepted bribe money from moonshiners was another question. I figured he had signed the same document Willie had to keep out of jail. Can't say I blamed him.

"That's all, Your Honor," Tavenner said. He walked to his seat and looked toward Timberlake.

"Mr. Timberlake, you may cross-examine," Judge Paul said.

Timberlake sauntered slowly toward Bridges and leaned on the railing between them as if what he had to say was confidential.

"You don't like Ewell Stuart very much, do you?" he said.

Bridges shrugged. "I don't have nothing special against him."

Next came Timberlake's slap across the face I wasn't expecting. "You were tried for murder in 1923, weren't you?"

Bridges bit the inside of his jaw before he snapped out his answer.

"You must know I was."

Timberlake stood ramrod straight, looked at the jury, and pointed to Bridges.

"You were tried for the murder of your own brother and brother-in-law, weren't you?"

Bridges coughed into his fist before answering. "Yes."

"Didn't you make the statement that you didn't care a damn what happened to the Stuart family because James Stuart, Ewell Stuart's father, had prosecuted you too hard?"

Bridges shrugged his right shoulder. "I don't remember saying that, but that was the way I felt."

When Timberlake finished his questioning, the judge called for a twenty-minute recess. I wanted to talk to Willie, needed to find some water, and was in desperate want of fresh air. But I had to avoid the pesky reporters and especially wanted to protect her from them.

I worked my way up the aisle to where she was sitting and pointed toward a side door. Most people were filtering out the front and we needed some breathing room. I led the way and she followed in my wake. Outside we stood in the shade of an evergreen. She looked prettier than I'd ever seen her, and I told her so. If you didn't know her, you wouldn't imagine she was a high-speed bootleg driver, and I was sure she'd impress the jury.

"Any idea when you'll be called to testify?" I asked her.

"Sam White's next, I think. I may be up by late afternoon or tomorrow morning."

I gave her a look of concern. "How are you holding up?"

"Doesn't matter, does it? I don't have a choice except to hold myself together." She tried to smile and failed.

"Matters to me," I said.

"Jimmy," she said turning her face up to mine, "I never meant to do harm to anyone."

"I know."

"I meant only to give people what they wanted for their enjoyment." She looked at the needles of the evergreen, and I saw she was drifting into her own thoughts. "It doesn't make sense, does it? The law won't allow us to sell liquor but punishes us for not giving them a share when we do. It's— it's—"

"Hypocritical?" I offered.

"Downright wicked," she corrected.

I laughed. "Yes, wicked's a better word, sister."

24.
Willie — April 1935

When the trial resumed, Tavenner called Samuel O. White to the stand. I wasn't surprised he was a witness for the government. Tall and thin, White wore wire-rim glasses and pressed his mouth in a serious line. He swore to tell the truth, as did the others, but I wasn't sure he would be true to his word.

After White settled himself in the witness chair, Tavenner made him wait before he began questioning. White started to sweat and pulled a handkerchief from his coat pocket to wipe his cheek. It surely was hot, and I felt a trickle of perspiration roll down my spine. I slipped a piece of paper from my purse and fanned myself with it — notes I had thought to bring in case I needed details to use during my testimony.

Finally, the attorney started.

"Mr. White, did you participate in the alleged whiskey conspiracy?"

White answered quickly and firmly. "No, sir."

When the questions and answers came rapid fire, I could tell Tavenner was a skilled investigator.

"Did you ever afford protection from the law to anyone?"

Again, a quick answer. "No, sir."

"Did you ever accept payment of money from anyone in the liquor business?"

"Not a cent."

Tavenner strolled to his desk and craned his neck toward a piece of paper lying there. Then he turned back to White.

"Would you tell the jury what you have done in the performance of your duty as an officer of the law?"

White lifted his chin. He must have memorized statistics and gave a half smile as if he was proud to recite them.

"From 1925 through 1932, I participated in destroying over six hundred stills, more than twenty thousand gallons of whiskey, and in excess of a million and a half gallons of mash, most of it in Franklin County. I helped to arrest two hundred five persons and seize one hundred and three vehicles. I have aided in the capture of a hundred twenty liquor cars with thirty-six hundred gallons of whiskey as cargo."

"I see." Tavenner showed no expression at his witness's preparation. I knew it was what he expected. "What has been your association with known bootleggers?"

White again lifted his chin as if assured he had committed no offense. His voice had a superior tone as if to say *how dare you accuse me*.

"I held frequent conferences with them at any place and time they named. The sole purpose for such meetings was to secure tips to advance my law enforcement activities. There was no other motive."

Tavenner spoke to White while his eyes scanned the jury.

"Some men have said that you told Willie Carter Sharpe where you were going to be and when to stay off the road."

"That is absolutely not true," White snapped.

I wanted to yell out that was a damned lie, but I wouldn't call attention to myself.

"Didn't you accept fifty dollars from Ewell Stuart for catching Willie Carter Sharpe?"

I felt a chill at hearing my name. White jerked his head to the side before he spoke, obviously resenting the question.

"I was in Stuart's office when he offered the fifty dollars to anyone who would capture her. A week later Bridges and I caught her and tried to force Stuart to make good. It took a year and a half."

A shiver shook me. I remembered that day as if it were yesterday. How they found me, I have no idea. There is a sense, a shudder animals feel before disaster hits. They know ahead of a flood to move to high ground. Their ears perk up before thunder rolls. I had watched Coochie crouch down on the Ford's seat even before I knew I was going to make a sharp turn to dodge a copper. If we're aware enough, if our senses are alert enough, we feel what's coming before we hear or smell or see it. I had the sensation as I put on my shoes in my room that evening, as I pulled on a sweater and checked my hair in the mirror. In the reflection I saw White and Bridges looking over my shoulder. A person can't hide forever. Although I rarely came out during daylight, it was getting on to evening and I needed to get some food into me and clear my lungs with clean air. It was dusk and ribbons of pink streaked the sky, setting the river aglow like seething embers. I didn't recognize the car parked outside my boarding house, but I knew who was in it. When they saw me, they opened the doors, got out, and glared at me. I had no inclination to run. I was relieved, really, to stop running, to obey their order to go inside and pack a bag as they waited like gentleman callers. When I returned, Bridges took my bag. White held open the car door for me. They asked if I was hungry because we had a long drive ahead. They didn't put me in cuffs—they were confident I wouldn't be violent or make a run for it. Bridges carried a gun, and I had no desire to take a bullet in the back. Anyway, my freedom had left me years ago when I moved away from Pop's place in Silver Ridge. What was freedom, anyway, but an end of one thing and the beginning of another? Freedom was waiting for something to happen, and in White's car, I knew the wait was over.

I brought my attention back to the courtroom where Tavenner had White cornered.

"Did you not know it is a violation of law to accept a gratuity in the performance of your duty?" he asked.

"No, I did not and I didn't accept it in that way," White said. "It was only to have some fun out of Ewell Stuart. Federal agents in West Virginia were splitting fees with state officers and everyone knew it."

Judge Paul broke in. "Don't you know that splitting fees with state officers is contrary to law?"

"No, sir," White said.

I had a hard time understanding how a federal agent could be so ignorant of the law. But the charge of splitting fees was petty, and Tavenner changed the subject. He was going after bigger fish.

"Have you heard anything about Ewell Stuart accepting payments from bootleggers?"

"I don't think it would have been any of my business to investigate Mr. Stuart even if he'd been taking graft. That would have been up to the governor of Virginia."

White's tongue snaked out to lick his lips. The tongue quivered. He was nervous, all right, but he wasn't finished.

"I've heard rumors about officers ever since I've been in the service—the longer a man's been in the service the more crooked he becomes, according to some people. Stuart always cooperated with me one hundred percent."

Timberlake had no questions for White, letting him off the hook. When it was his turn to call a witness for the defense, he drew an ace card. First he ducked his head and whispered something to Stuart. Then he stood and said, "I call Ewell Stuart, Commonwealth's Attorney for Franklin County."

Back straight, Stuart appeared taller than he was. He carried his ancestors on his shoulders—generals and heroes, distinguished in their own right. Settling into the chair, he laid a hand on the railing in front of him as if to say he owned the courthouse and everyone in it.

"Mr. Stuart," Timberlake began, "have you ever entered into any conspiracy to defraud the government by fostering the manufacturing and sale of illicit whiskey?"

"No, sir," Stuart answered. "To the contrary, I've always done what I could to prevent bootlegger liquor being manufactured and sold." His voice assumed the authority of a man pledging allegiance to the flag, except there was not a word of truth to what he said. What he meant was if he couldn't prevent moonshine from being made and sold, then he'd make his own profit from it. The devil's in the details, I've always heard.

Tavenner rubbed his jaw in a thoughtful manner before he asked the next question.

"Mr. Stuart, do you know of an old tradition of making whiskey in Franklin County, Virginia?"

Stuart wasted no time in answering, an answer everyone in Southwest Virginia knew.

"Liquor has been made and sold in Franklin County for generations. Stopping it was difficult, especially in the mountains. There's an ingrained determination of the people to make whiskey. If they hanged everyone they caught making it, they'd still make it."

Stuart was right—the Union declared their victory in the Civil War, but the Confederates weren't about to finance their government by paying a tax on their own liquor. You could bet a century from now there would still be moonshine stills in Southwest Virginia.

"What is your record in liquor cases, Mr. Stuart?" Timberlake said.

"I've had four-hundred-seventy-five convictions. I have been so active as a prosecutor that the jail often was running over."

Stuart gave the impression he'd had his hands full. I supposed that work included drinking the local product in the office of Blackwater Filling Station with Bridges. I had to smile when Timberlake asked, "You've been a busy man, Mr. Stuart?"

"Yes, sir. I've had all the work I could do. Even worked at night to keep up. People call me about everything from somebody's chickens disappearing to murder."

Timberlake turned his smile toward the jury as if asking them to acknowledge Stuart's little joke. Then he returned to Stuart.

"Have you ever been paid for protection of a still?"

When Stuart answered the question, I hoped Timberlake would remind him he was under oath.

"I never received any money except for a fine."

He was mincing words. Stuart didn't collect fines—it was payoff. Then he had the men hauled off to jail anyway.

"Was it difficult to prosecute liquor cases?"

I figured Stuart had prepared his answers to Timberlake's questions ahead of the trial. The lawyer must have fed him the script.

"Unless we could prove that a man was actually at work at a still, it was nigh next to impossible to get a conviction," Stuart said. "Persons at the still almost invariably said they were simply passing by or they were there to get a drink of cider. Bootleggers knew the cars of the local officers and used telephones to warn each other. Blackwater Filling Station was raided so many times I couldn't recall the number."

Timberlake was an actor reciting his memorized lines. He was so relaxed asking the questions I thought he looked a mite bored. Or maybe that was the impression he wanted to give the jury.

"What was your experience with liquor cars?"

Stuart wasted no time answering. "More than two hundred automobiles were seized for liquor violations in my term of office, and more than one hundred were sold at auction, mostly to bootleggers." He jerked his head back and forth. "I wouldn't have a car a bootlegger had driven. They were shot pretty well to pieces as a rule."

I'd been shot at, sure, and the cars bore the scars. If I had Charlie to thank for anything, it was the way he reinforced the Ford's chassis.

"There has been testimony of your receiving payments of protection money from bootleggers," Timberlake said. "Are those statements true?"

I could have predicted Stuart's answer.

"I never received any such payments."

I reckoned if you were descended from a southern war hero, you could you get away with telling a boldfaced lie to a judge and jury and they'd all swallow it. Truth be told, I wouldn't trust Stuart to speak the truth to his own mother.

When Timberlake was finished with Stuart, Judge Paul ordered Tavenner to call his next witness. Tavenner stood and said in a loud and formal voice, "The prosecution calls Charles Sharpe to the stand."

It was all I could do to keep from jumping up, pointing a finger at Charlie, and calling him out for being a rogue, a cheat, and a wolf. I flicked my head around to see if the woman he called his wife was in the room but with the shock of learning about her, I couldn't recall what she looked like. A cheap hussy, if anything. I turned around and held my head still but my eyes scanned the jury, scanned Tavenner, scanned Charlie. He had on a shirt so white it must have been new, and he looked like a gangly teenager with a tie in a sloppy knot at his neck. When the questioning began, I squeezed my hands together in my lap. Stay calm, Willie, I told myself. From somewhere the words of a song stuck in my head. What was it—weeping at remembering a life gone by? Something like that. Well, there would be no weeping today, not for Charlie Sharpe anyway. I hoped he'd get his due.

"Mr. Sharpe," Tavenner said, "you are acquainted with Willie Carter Sharpe?"

I leaned forward. Tavenner didn't tell me I'd come up in Charlie's questioning.

"Willie Carter—no Sharpe." Charlie shifted his eyes toward me. His face wasn't hateful, but now we were playing on different teams.

"Were you ever married to Willie Carter?"

Charlie stifled a smile. "No."

"But you lived together?"

"She lived with me for a time, yes."

I heaved a deep sigh. Charlie was wrong—we were as good as married. Any couple thinking about having a baby was every bit as good as married. Sixty or seventy years ago if a couple couldn't get to a church or a town hall or a preacher, they lived together and provided for each other and nobody raised an eyebrow. It's the Catholic Church that changed things by calling it living in sin. If we had lived in one of those states allowing common law marriage, we'd have been recognized as man and wife. But the best moonshine came from Virginia, so that's where we needed to be, common-law marriage or not.

Tavenner kept the questions coming. Simple questions with simple answers.

"For how long did you live with Willie?"

"I don't know. A time."

A time? *Charlie, my heart shudders to hear you make light of those nights in our bed, your bare skin against mine. Tell the lawyer how you moaned with pleasure when you entered me and my hips rose to meet yours, drawing you deeper inside me, my fingers clawing your back. Tell him how our breaths came ragged and desperate, how you brought me to the peak of an ecstasy forged in heaven. Then have him ask again if we were married. Had I loved you, Charlie? Yes, I loved you as far as I understood love, and now I weep at remembering that life – all gone by.*

I felt in my bag for a handkerchief and brought it to my nose.

"Try to be specific, please," Tavenner said.

"All right. She lived with me five years, I'd guess."

Five years – most of them happy. It was in the fifth year that I made the left turn to this day, and Charlie was a man who couldn't be without a woman when his woman was in jail.

"And were you hauling liquor during that time?"

Charlie looked up at the judge. "I don't believe I need to answer that question."

"I believe you do," Tavenner said.

Judge Paul resolved the standoff. "Answer the question, Mr. Sharpe, and remember you are under oath."

Charlie sighed and gave his head a side-to-side shudder. I wondered whether the judge had absolved him of guilt to get his testimony. If not, Charlie was looking at jail time.

"I started hauling in 1928 and continued until 1931," he said.

"And how often would you haul a load of liquor?" Tavenner asked.

"I'd make two or three trips a week."

Charlie was wrong. We hauled nearly every night. And nearly every night we made love to each other. I squeezed the handkerchief in my hand. No weeping.

"How much liquor, on average, in each haul?"

"An average of one hundred gallons a load, I'd guess."

"And where did the gallons of liquor originate?"

As if Tavenner didn't know. But he needed to get Charlie's answer on the record, I figured.

"In Franklin County."

"Did you use a pilot when you drove?"

"Didn't need one. No other car could keep up with my speedster."

Was Charlie protecting me? It was common knowledge I piloted for him—and for others, too. I drew up my shoulders, trying not to be tense as a rabbit staring down a snake.

Tavenner crossed his arms over his chest as if he was asking a question he was curious about, not one he already knew the answer to. "Have you ever been arrested for hauling illegal liquor?"

Charlie shrugged. "Sure, I done some time like anybody else. Been shot at, too, but I generally carried enough cash to pay my way through a roadblock."

"I see." I thought he'd ask who Charlie paid, how much, how often. Instead, Tavenner looked at some papers in his hand, then said to the judge, "No more questions, Your Honor."

25.
Jimmy — April 1935

As I listened to Charlie Sharpe's testimony, I remembered that Virginia had never recognized common law marriage. No matter how many years you lived together, you had to sign a marriage license to be considered man and wife. Dottie would never have considered living with me without that sheet of paper. She was like that and I guess I was, too. Doing things by the book, I mean. My sister was different. If there was a way to get around a law she considered senseless, she'd find that route and take it the same way she avoided the police on her night runs. I found it strange that she'd take Charlie's name, though. She wanted nothing more to do with the Carters, as if adding Sharpe to her name erased those years with Floyd. She'd never be free of the Carters, though. They were, after all, the ones who got her into the bootleg business that led her here to this courthouse and put her at even greater risk.

Tavenner called Willie to the stand, and the clerk swore her in as Willie Carter Sharpe. If Charlie Sharpe didn't acknowledge her as his wife, at least the court did. Bootleggers were used to lying to protect themselves. Willie told me once when she was stopped she made up a story about her husband being chief of police in a city in South Carolina, of all things. She had been visiting an aging aunt, she told the officer, and had gotten word her husband had been in a car accident and was badly injured. She was on her way south to see about him and was very sorry about speeding. The officer told her his men had blocked a bridge up ahead to catch rum runners and instead of arresting her for carrying liquor, he sent one of his men to open the bridge for her.

Willie knew how to lie, but I believed under oath she'd hold to the truth. She held her head high when she stepped into the witness box. She and Tavenner had made an agreement, and it wasn't Willie he was out to get.

Tavenner's voice got softer when he spoke to her.

"State your name, please," he said.

"Willie Sharpe."

I was surprised she left Carter's name out. I guessed Tavenner was, too.

"Is it Mrs. Willie Carter Sharpe?" he said.

"Yes, sir."

Tavenner didn't mention Charlie's testimony. Virginia didn't require drivers to carry licenses until 1932, so Willie was free to call herself whatever she wanted. I supposed it didn't matter to the law what she named herself. What mattered was helping Tavenner win his case.

"What is your age?"

"Thirty-two."

My sister was all of thirty-two? I was twenty-eight, so I guess that was about right. Where had the time gone? We had been in a depression for six years, fought a world war, seen two great ships sink, and lost our mother to a cancer. For all of it, I felt so much older. Willie probably did, too, especially wasting so many of those years behind bars.

"Where do you live?" Obviously Tavenner was trying to get the basic facts into the record.

"I'm staying at my father's in Floyd County at the present time," she said.

Pop wasn't doing much farming since May died, but I knew he enjoyed Willie's company. I hoped she was doing some cooking for him. He was skin and bone.

Next the hard questions came. "When did you first begin to take part in the liquor business?"

"You mean hauling it, transporting it?"

"Yes, in Franklin County."

"In 1927."

That was two years before the crash. People had plenty of money for liquor in those days. She was barely twenty-four then.

"Please tell the jury in what way you worked and for whom," Tavenner said.

Willie set her mouth and looked out at the spectators before she answered.

"When I first started hauling liquor, I hauled some myself and then started piloting."

She didn't mention Floyd Carter or driving for his father, John Carter. The old man was dead now, probably from drinking too much of his own liquor, and Floyd was never involved in driving. I got the impression Floyd was simple, so his father put him in charge of checking on the stills and enforcing punishment on anyone who meddled with business.

"Tell the jury what you mean by piloting."

Willie laced her fingers together and planted them in her lap. She must have been nervous, but she was determined to do what Tavenner had asked of her.

"Well, in piloting a liquor car, somebody has to drive one car that doesn't have any liquor in it. Someone else always drove the liquor car, and I protected it."

"In what way would you protect it?"

Willie easily knew the answer to this question, having piloted hundreds—maybe thousands of times.

"I had to outrun the law or act as a decoy and lead the law on a wild goose chase to distract them," she said. "Most of the time it was in Roanoke County, sometimes Franklin County."

"When you were piloting those cars, would you ever pilot more than one car at a time?"

"Yes sir. Piloted as many as ten. Different drivers, different nights, but they all wanted a good pilot."

"You mean to say you have piloted as many as ten cars loaded with liquor?"

"Some loaded at Blackwater Filling Station, some at Ferrum." She gave a little shrug. "I was the only one there to help them."

I hadn't been aware my sister had worked so hard. There must have been long nights for her. She was a better driver than I knew.

"How were you paid?" Tavenner said.

"Most of them gave me ten dollars."

"When you had these ten cars, they gave you ten dollars apiece? That was very profitable."

"It was my neck on the line, too. I couldn't do it for nothing."

Good answer, sister, I thought.

"When you were hauling liquor, where were you hauling from?"

"From Roosevelt Smith's and Peg Hatcher's. I think his given name was Walter, but we always called him Peg."

"Did Peg Hatcher or Roosevelt Smith ever say anything to you about the county officers letting you alone, that they would not bother you?"

"They told me—" She stumbled, and I wondered if she could get the words out.

"Go ahead, Mrs. Sharpe," Tavenner said.

Willie took a breath and let it out. "They told me I wouldn't have any trouble with the law as long as the whiskey came from them."

"I see." Tavenner studied the floor as if organizing a thought and then turned again to Willie. "Did they ever state that they were paying money to anyone to safeguard you?"

Here was the crux of the matter, the question that would put Peg and Roose in jail. Willie had to be careful about how she answered.

"I heard them talking. They said they had to pay so much to keep the roads clear in order to get the whiskey out of Franklin County."

Tavenner nodded. He seemed pleased with Willie's answer.

"Now," he said, "I want you to tell this jury if you know of any connections that Ewell Stuart has had with the enforcement or the failure to enforce the Prohibition laws in Franklin county, to your own knowledge."

Tavenner was out to get Stuart, that was sure. Willie blinked toward Stuart and her hands fidgeted.

"There's lots of talk. I couldn't be positive. About the only thing I know is that Roosevelt told me if anybody got caught in Rocky Mount he could get them out of it. That's about the only thing I could tell the truth about."

Well done, sister. If she had accused Stuart of wrongdoing, he might have come after her to the ends of the earth.

"Did he mention any particular officer as being one he could fix it up with?"

"He said he could make it all right with Stuart. That's all he said—he could fix it with Stuart."

There it was—Willie's head on Stuart's chopping block. Even from a prison cell he'd get his cronies to hunt her down.

"Tell the jury when you were hauling liquor about how much liquor you hauled from Roosevelt Smith's since 1928," Tavenner said.

Willie hesitated, figuring.

"It's all right, Mrs. Sharpe. Just tell the jury the truth," Tavenner said.

"I usually hauled every day of the year, so you can figure it out."

"It was almost a daily matter with you?"

"Yes sir. Sometimes two or three times a day."

"How much liquor would you haul at a load?"

"Sometimes one-ten, sometimes one-fifty."

"One hundred ten and one hundred fifty gallons?"

"Yes, sir."

"Would you go even on Sunday?"

"Yes, sir."

"How in the world would Roosevelt Smith or Peg Hatcher have a load or several loads of liquor practically every day for you?"

I was asking myself that question. My sister hauled four hundred gallons of liquor a day? The bosses must have kept those distillers busy all night long.

"They kept it stored around where they could get it," Willie said. "They've had as much as two or three thousand gallons setting around at a time."

"Do you know where they got the liquor?"

"I guess they bought it from moonshiners."

Tavenner rubbed his chin and seemed to be contemplating the far wall. I believed he was trying to create a sense of drama, and Willie's answer provided what he was going for.

"Mrs. Sharpe, you have been requested to make an estimate of the number of gallons of liquor which you purchased from or piloted through Peg Hatcher, Roosevelt Smith, and J. O. Shively. Have you prepared such a statement?"

"I estimated that the best I could. It's guesswork."

"Will you read your list to the jury, please?"

Willie unfolded a paper and began to read.

"Peg Hatcher from 1927 to May 11, 1931, at least sixty-five thousand gallons. Roosevelt Smith from 1927 to May 11, 1931, at least sixty-five thousand gallons. J. O. Shively from 1927 to May 11, 1931, at least ten thousand gallons." She stopped and looked up at Tavenner. "Most of my work was piloting. Some drivers have moved more than a million gallons. I haven't hauled so awful much myself."

I felt my mouth fall open. I knew moonshine was big business in Virginia, but I hadn't realized how big. Or how deep Willie was involved.

Tavenner walked up to the witness stand and put his hands on the rail as if what he had to say next was between the two of them and no one else.

"Now, Mrs. Sharpe, you had interactions with Deputy Sheriff Jeff Richards. Is that correct?"

I swear I saw Willie's cheeks pink. When she said, "I knew him, yes," I heard a quiver in her voice. She'd told me about Richards, about their—relationship.

"On some occasions you met Mr. Richards after a run of liquor, didn't you?"

"I met with him a few times."

"On one of those nights, you and Mr. Richards stopped in front of a store to count money he had collected, did you not?"

"I may recall that."

Willie kept her answers short and to the point. If Tavenner wanted more, he'd dig it out of her.

"Do you remember how much money Mr. Richards had collected that night?"

"I believe it was eight-hundred-twenty-five dollars."

"And where did he say he got that large an amount of money?"

"He told me it came from Franklin County distillers and whiskey dealers."

"I see." Here Tavenner turned from Willie and faced the jury. "And what did he say he intended to do with the money?"

Again Willie shifted her eyes to Stuart. I was afraid my sister was inviting her own death sentence.

"It was to be divided between Ewell Stuart and himself. I got twenty-five dollars of it."

Tavenner turned to Willie with a quizzical expression.

"Why did he give you twenty-five dollars?"

"That's one question I wouldn't like to answer."

Tavenner waited until the muttering among the spectators calmed down. He wasn't finished.

"You and Richards were rather close friends, weren't you?"

"Yes, sir." Willie's voice was weak, and she studied her hands.

"Then you knew he was murdered two weeks before this trial commenced?"

Now she lifted her eyes. Her friend — her lover, if that's what he was — had been done wrong.

"I heard they shot him fifty times," she said.

Several people gasped and a woman's voice said, "Fifty?" followed by a thunder of murmurs. Judge Paul banged his gavel on the desk.

It had been all over the front pages. One week before the federal grand jury returned its conspiracy indictment, Deputy Sheriff Thomas Jefferson Richards was gunned down in his car along with a prisoner on a country road. Whoever put fifty bullets in him surely wanted him dead. No witnesses stepped forward and no one confessed. Richards had told people that he expected to go to prison but would not go alone, and many believed — including me — he was killed to keep him from testifying. Willie had grown fond of him, so she said. Not love — far from it. And not even close to the feelings she had for Charlie Sharpe. But they had respected each other, and

Richards protected her from getting arrested again, at least in Franklin County. Saint Louis was out of his jurisdiction. But it wasn't out of White's.

Tavenner turned toward the faces in the courtroom seats. One of them, no doubt, was Mrs. Richards.

"And I'm sure you will join with me in sending condolences to his wife," he said.

"Sure I do," Willie answered.

Willie must have known about Richards having a wife, or maybe she didn't care. Being married obviously hadn't bothered him and for Willie, her relationship with Richards was more a business deal than romance.

Tavenner started to his table. "That will be all, Your Honor," he said. He had done his work. Willie had been believable, but Tavenner had broken a few hearts that morning.

• • •

Following Willie's testimony, I took a few days off from the trial. I had to get back to work, but in the evenings I visited Pop and usually found Willie there. I always brought Coochie with me, and both Willie and the dog wept joyful tears when they saw each other.

Willie was so well known by now that reporters hounded her even as far as Floyd County. Pop kept his shotgun loaded to scare them off. I knew he didn't like what she had become and neither did I, but we were family. I was glad May wasn't around to see it. But Willie was still his daughter, and he had a right to protect her even if it meant filling an intruder's backside full of buckshot.

One night she made a navy bean soup with salt pork and cornbread. I liked sugar in my cornbread with apple butter spread on it, the way Dottie made it, but Willie said white people took their cornbread without sugar. That was May's recipe, too, but I found an old jar of May's apple butter in the pantry and spread it liberally on my square of the cornbread. Pop said he liked it either way.

Another evening Willie set a platter of fried chicken on the table.

"Where'd you get the bird?" I asked, my mouth watering.

"Remember when May used to go out to the scurry of hens, chase one down and wring its neck with a quick twist?"

"Of course," I said, "and she'd take the hatchet, lay the chicken on a stump, and make quick work of it."

Willie nodded. "Well, I was thinking of May." She pushed the platter toward me. "Let's see if I've done her justice with frying it up."

Pop bit into a thigh and agreed Willie had honored her mother. In fact, I believed Willie's fried chicken beat Dottie's, but I wouldn't tell Dottie that. Maybe it had something to do with sitting at Pop's table and the memories of being twelve and always hungry, barely able to wait until suppertime to dig into May's home cooking. I missed May, but I had my own family now and a man can't go back. He's got to keep moving forward. I hoped Willie realized she had to move forward, too.

After we ate, Willie got up and cleared the plates then came back with a rock in her palm.

"What've you got there?" I said. She held out her hand. It was a bumpy rock that looked like it had the pox.

"Must've been thrown up from the last plowing." She rubbed the ash-colored thing as if it was Aladdin's lamp. "I think it's one of those with crystals inside. Quartz or amethyst maybe."

"Let me see that." When she handed it to me, its heaviness surprised me. I turned the rock around, studying its globe shape. "I've seen stones like this before. Let's smash it open and see what's inside." I looked to Pop. "Where are you keeping your hammer?"

Willie snatched back the rock from my hand. "I know what's inside. You smash it and prove me wrong, I'll never forgive you. Let me believe what I believe."

"Suit yourself," I said. Willie didn't have much left to trust, and if she wanted to believe her piece of rock held a treasure, who was I to shatter her faith?

It was good to talk about chickens and rocks and anything besides the trial. We didn't touch on the Big Question, either, which was where Willie was going to go once the trial was over. If reporters kept at her, the Bondurants, the most famous bootleg family in the state, and other distillers out to get her for being a turncoat would surely track her down and punish her—maybe even kill her. It was hard for me to think of my sister as a criminal. But I reckoned that's what she had become. Trouble was, she was a criminal on both sides of the law.

When a dog is injured, it hides near the house until it heals or dies. It doesn't come no matter how much you call it. But staying near the farm was too dangerous for Willie. And she wouldn't be able to find honest work anywhere in Roanoke— not even in all of Virginia. Kentucky bootleggers would be after her, too. I doubted she could handle the cold up north and didn't have the credentials to get into Canada. It looked like moving west was her best bet. She settled in Saint Louis and if Sam White didn't give away her whereabouts, she might be able to stay awhile.

26.
Willie — May 1935

Pop drove me to the courthouse one afternoon because I wanted to sit in on the trial of Thomas Rakes. He said he wasn't about to go in with that crowd — might catch some disease from all those people. He'd walk around town, get a newspaper, and wait for me in the park. A gal gets confidence from knowing her pa is nearby even if he's not at her elbow. There were damn few things I could count on at this point in my life, but Pop was one of them. I was grateful for him.

I had driven for Rakes early in the business and knew him as a fellow who didn't mince words. If Tavenner asked Rakes a question, I believed Rakes would give it to him straight. I thought Tavenner might be taking a risk asking Rakes to testify for the prosecution but Rakes, like the others, was trying to save his own hide.

Rakes was a tall fellow with sharp cheekbones and a predator's look to his eye. He wore a narrow string tie around the neck of a striped shirt, and a sport coat drooped over his bony frame. The clerk asked him to remove his fedora, and when he took it off I saw his hair was thinning. He ran a hand over his head before he raised his right arm at the elbow to be sworn in.

Once on the witness stand, Rakes looked ready to leap over the railing at anyone who contradicted him, but Tavenner was in charge and approached him the same way he had approached me.

"What is your occupation, Mr. Rakes?" he asked.

"Electrical contractor in Roanoke," Rakes said. He must have done the wiring for new houses, a job that required some intelligence and exactitude.

"Have you any connection with the liquor business?" Tavenner pressed.

"After I finished a contract and couldn't find any other work, I decided to make me some money running liquor," he said.

Rakes's answer was honest, but there was no point in lying now. Besides, everybody knew what he'd been up to. A man had to eat and put a roof over his head. As I knew too well, so did a woman.

Tavenner addressed Rakes but looked at the jury when he asked his next question.

"You knew, of course, that you were engaged in an illegal operation?"

That's when Rakes got his hackles up.

"Anyone can tell you the law can't legislate morality, and it certainly can't stop people from drinking."

Tavenner interrupted him. "We are interrogating witnesses based on a charge of conspiracy, Mr. Rakes." His voice had a warning in it. He wanted Rakes to stick to their script. I knew Rakes was unpredictable.

"The illegal liquor trade is worth tens of billions of dollars," Rakes said. "You want to charge someone, don't charge Willie Carter Sharpe—charge Al Capone and the other gangsters."

It shocked me to think Rakes would stand up for me. But why shouldn't he? I'd done a good job piloting for him, and he knew I was above board. I never accepted a cent I hadn't earned.

He swept his hand across the room. "I heard Capone makes over a hundred dollars a minute from illegal alcohol. Franklin County is small potatoes."

Now Rakes spoke to the jury, his brows furrowed. "I was raised in Franklin County and started making and hauling liquor like everyone else. You going to put the whole county in jail?"

Rakes had a point, and from the undertone of voices from those sitting in the courthouse seats, I could tell people got that point. I was sure every one of us sitting in the courthouse that afternoon had made or bought or transported illegal liquor and had shared it with neighbors—maybe even the judge himself. It wasn't selling bootleg whiskey that was costing the government so much money—it was this good-for-nothing trial.

Tavenner telling me I was never to drive again put a hardship on me, but he didn't say whether he meant I couldn't drive for bootleggers or drive any vehicle at any time. Of course, the state of Virginia wouldn't give me a driver's license with all my convictions but, Lord, I missed driving. It was like telling a concert pianist she could never play the keyboard again or telling an opera singer to keep her mouth shut. When you're good at something and you're denied the right to do that something, it's like losing a limb. The law had stolen the crown from the Queen of the Roanoke Rum Runners. All I had left were memories of putting the Ford through its paces and hopes of one day being behind the wheel again.

27.
Jimmy — June 1935

I didn't want to miss the attorneys' closing arguments and thought it best to drive Willie to the courthouse the morning of the trial's last day. We arrived at the courthouse early on the last Friday in June and found seats together near the front. Willie looked crisp in a checkered dress with what Dottie would call capped shoulders and a narrow belt at the waist. I suspected she was ready for this entire legal mess to be finished, no matter what the outcome.

For the next half hour, spectators filed in behind us, men relieved of their suit jackets against the early summer heat. Willie and I rose when Judge Paul entered, as the clerk instructed us. The judge looked tired. For two solid weeks the trial had been draining on him with emotions running high. The jury, too, had dragged themselves to their seats looking worn out, but most of them had their lips pressed together in determined expressions. This was their final act.

The judge banged his gavel to call the court to order and addressed the two attorneys.

"Gentleman, please deliver your closing comments. Mr. Tavenner, you may begin."

Tavenner had the look of a man who knew he had the case sewn up. His suit appeared pressed and his shoes polished. He moseyed to the jury box and addressed the men whose eyes drooped with fatigue.

"Sirs," Tavenner began, "the testimony of these witnesses clearly shows a connivance of officers with these bootleggers. Because of it these defendants have brought into the county quantities of materials that astound the imagination—and these officers come here and say they couldn't see it when its very shadow is apparent here in Roanoke, in Lynchburg, and it darkens your very doors." He pointed to several jurors who sat up straighter, as if the lawyer had poked them in the chest.

Tavenner swiveled toward the defendants' table and then back to the jury. "It has been established that sixty-two thousand pounds of yeast have been shipped into Franklin County. Manufactured into bread, the loaves, laid end to end, would stretch from Roanoke to Omaha, Nebraska." He swept out his arm to stress the distance. "In Franklin County alone, thirty-three million, seven-hundred-seventy pounds of sugar were used from 1930 until 1935. If spread out over the ten-acre city of Roanoke, it would be three-quarters of an inch deep."

I had to admire Tavenner's technique. He had a way of showing the extent of the moonshine business. Roanoke to Omaha had to be over a thousand miles. That would be a heap of bread loaves.

"The tax," he said, "on over a million gallons of liquor hauled out of Franklin County, and not including the two hundred thousand gallons credited to Willie Carter Sharpe—" Here he tossed a look at Willie. "—would amount to five and a half million dollars. If these defendants expect you to believe that they did not know it, then I say to you that it is a monument to ignorance."

Tavenner stretched an arm toward Stuart. "Attorney Stuart was in a position to know everything there was to be known about the conditions of delivering bootleg liquor."

He spoke again to the jury. "Picture, if you will, these officers conniving with bootleggers, sitting around the table drinking and dividing money collected. The money may not have been transferred hand to hand but would be laid down on a table, placed in the crack of a granary, put on the seat of an automobile or under a bottle in a barbershop." He swiped his index finger across the jury's line of vision as if dismissing a thought. "That nefarious business has continued until it has culminated in one of the greatest eras of crime that we know."

Tavenner paused and leaned on the railing of the jury box, searching the eye of each juror.

"It's time to give the county back to its people," he said.

I flashed a look at Willie. She was stone still. Even I couldn't read her face.

Judge Paul wrote a note on a piece of paper with a ballpoint pen. After Tavenner sat, the judge said, "Mr. Timberlake?"

Like Tavenner, Timberlake approached the jury box and spoke directly to the jurors. He hesitated a few seconds and then began as if his words came directly from his heart.

"Ewell Stuart comes from one of the most distinguished ancestries in America. His great uncle was the elder brother of the strongest, most reputable figure in Virginia history, who gave his life for the cause of our state's freedom."

I expected the defense attorney to speak well, but I didn't expect Jeb Stuart's very ghost to make an appearance. I should have known better. Timberlake knew he didn't have a good case, so he leaned on lineage.

"Having those qualities," he said, "Ewell Stuart could not possibly sink to the level that the government here claims. His every act has been brought out and put under scrutiny. Every hostility and hatred against him has been uncovered."

I reckoned not every act had been under scrutiny. Sure, he had turned in moonshiners selling their liquor, but he'd also profited from it. He had a big house, a big car, and a big ego.

But this was the south, and Timberlake must have known the south protected its own, whether their ancestors proved victorious in the Civil War or died trying.

"The very dregs of the underworld have been combed, and prison camps, jails, penitentiaries, and insane asylums have been combed so they could bring here thieves, rogues, and even murderers to parade across the witness stand and tell you that Ewell Stuart was engaged in a conspiracy. Whatever conspiracies existed in Franklin County, Ewell Stuart was not a member."

I wanted to stand and shout to Timberlake that my sister was not insane and she was not a thief. If he could win a case based on degrading the witnesses, then the rotten lawyer was pulling out all the stops. But he wasn't finished—he was going directly for Willie.

"As for Willie Carter Sharpe's claim against him, she was shown to be motivated by bias and hostility. No jury is going to attach much importance to the testimony of anyone who speaks from hatred. Mr. Stuart is the victim of a frame-up by government witnesses. I would do what you're going to do— close my ears against such testimony and refuse to convict even a yellow dog, much less a fellow human on such evidence."

I felt my hands ball into fists. Accusing Willie of speaking from hatred was downright low.

Timberlake pointed to Stuart. "I ask of you as a small measure of recompense to this boy for what he has suffered to reach a decision quickly and return him to his wife and baby and to the loving and loyal friends who await him."

The shrewd lawyer knew how to choose his words. Stuart was anything but a boy. He was at least a year older than I was. And with the word "baby," the attorney was relying on touching the hearts of the jurors instead of speaking to their sense of reason and good judgment. If this was how the law worked, I wanted nothing to do with it.

It sounded like Timberlake was wrapping up.

"The government contends that this is a very important case, but I say it is also important to these defendants. If they are acquitted, the government goes on, but if they are convicted, families will be broken up and suffering will follow." He shook a finger at the jury. "You hold these twenty-three men in the hollow of your hands."

At least in his final comments, I couldn't agree more with Timberlake. And with jobs being scarce because of the depression, I didn't know what their families would do if the judge ordered jail time for these men.

28.
Willie — July 1935

On Monday, July 1 — verdict day — the sun beat down on the courthouse. Inside, fans blew hot air on people jammed into every seat. Some women brought folding fans, men dabbed their faces with handkerchiefs, and others waved their necks with whatever paper they had on hand. I brought an accordion fan I found in May's dresser. Pop had cleaned out most of her things but had left a few items like a cologne bottle so her scent stayed in his bedroom and the fan she used when she sat on the porch on hot summer evenings. Judge Paul must have perspired under his black robe and gave permission for the attorneys to remove their suitcoats.

Jimmy stood at the back. Frank Tavenner had saved me a seat at the front, which I appreciated although after I sat down I felt eyes boring into my back and whispers of "That's Willie Carter Sharpe," "That's Willie," and "That's her."

After the judge took his seat, members of the jury filed in slow as sloths and filled the jury box. The judge addressed the twelve men directly.

"Jury, the charges for the twenty-three defendants in this case involve participating in a massive conspiracy to deprive the federal government of its proper venues — the taxes due on the manufacture of distilled spirits. Have you reached a verdict?"

The juror at the end of the first row stood up—the head juror, I supposed.

"We have your honor," he said.

The judge gazed out at the spectators. "What is your decision?"

By his receding hair, I reckoned the juror to be somewhere between my age and Pop's. He handed two sheets of paper to the clerk. For all the tension in the room, there might as well have been a rattler curled and ready to strike. I could almost hear its tail shake. The judge must have felt it, too.

"I warn the courtroom against any demonstration or outburst on the reading of the verdict," the judge said, and he adjusted the glasses on his nose.

The clerk proceeded to read the verdict.

"The jury finds the following guilty—"

I listened for the names of men I knew, Samuel O. White, Walter Hatcher, alias "Peg" Hatcher, Roosevelt Smith, Willard Hodges, J. O. Shively. There were a dozen other names, but I had borne witness against these people I knew well. They would blame me for sending them to jail even though they didn't deserve a minute behind bars. I hoped they wouldn't hold it against me when they got out. The clerk hadn't mentioned Charlie Sharpe. Charlie was as guilty as the rest of them, but Tavenner must have gotten him a pardon for testifying.

The clerk's next words caused a loud hum from the spectators.

"The jury finds the following not guilty: Will Wray, Howard L. Maxey, and Ewell Stuart."

I hadn't mentioned Wray and Maxey in my testimony, but I shifted in my seat when I heard Stuart was acquitted. I knew as well as every person who ever took a drink in Franklin County that the Commonwealth's attorney was as guilty as sin itself.

Whether the judge was pleased with the outcome or not, he called for quiet amid the buzz in the courtroom and then thanked the jury.

"You have performed your duties well and have carried out my instructions to the letter," he said. "Your performance has served to renew my belief in the American justice system."

Maybe the judge's belief in carrying out the law was renewed, but to prohibit the selling of liquor and locking up men who've tried to scratch a living from their own hard work was, in my belief, not only unfair — it was downright senseless.

The clerk asked us to rise from our seats while Judge Paul left his desk. As the jury filtered out, Tavenner turned to me and held out his hand. I accepted his handshake although I wasn't feeling I'd done anything that needed congratulating.

"You did good, Willie," he said.

Ewell Stuart slowed down when he walked by and gave me a toothy smile of victory.

"Not good enough, I suppose."

"You'd better keep your nose clean from now on and stay out of automobiles," Tavenner said.

"That's asking a lot." I wasn't sure whether the bitterness stinging me was for the lawyer or for myself for selling out to him.

Tavenner frowned. "I mean it, Willie. There's some that are going to have it out for you."

"Tell me something I don't know." I thought of Jeff Richards, the flash of light he saw as a rain of bullets came at him, lead cracking his skull, bursting his heart in mid-beat, splattering his blood across the car's seat.

The lawyer picked up his briefcase. "Best of luck to you, Willie," he said.

I'd need more than luck. Judging from the look Stuart gave me, I'd need a cape of invisibility.

Outside, I found Jimmy standing by a group gathered around Ewell Stuart. Reporters with notebooks and cameras threw questions at him.

"What are you going to do now, Mr. Stuart?" one asked.

"I'm running for reelection as the Commonwealth's Attorney." Stuart was making an announcement, speaking slowly enough for the reporters to get every word down on their pads of paper. "And if elected I will discharge the duties of that office honestly, vigorously, and impartially."

Sure, I thought—as vigorously and honestly as you pocketed money from moonshiners. As impartially as you sat in Jo Shively's office playing poker and drinking the whiskey he had stored there.

"Willie." Jimmy jerked his head toward the courthouse steps. "That's Richards's widow."

The woman was dressed in black with a black hat, a veil across her eyes. She glared at me, a look of recognition and grief. I saw another aspect to her face, too, a hint of forgiveness and an understanding that we had something in common. What was the point of holding a grudge when we'd both been with a certain fellow and neither of us could keep him from being shot to death?

She walked by without speaking.

29.
Jimmy — March 1936

I hadn't heard word one from Willie in months. Not a phone call, a letter, or even a telegram. Maybe she was living in Saint Louis again.

"I've got to find her," I told Dottie. "She might be in trouble."

"Then we're going with you," she said. I didn't think Dottie liked Willie. Or maybe didn't approve of her is a better way to put it. Being a woman, she must have sensed what Willie was going through, losing her livelihood, her lover, her home. Dottie had a tender heart, and she knew I wouldn't rest until I found Willie.

"What about Coochie?" I said.

"Coochie can come, too," Dottie said. "The boys will take care of her."

I nodded. Coochie was an old dog now, but she might help us find Willie. "Pack warm clothes. It's bound to be chilly."

We stuffed sweaters and toothbrushes into overnight bags and Dottie loaded a sack with snacks. Then George and Archie raced Coochie to the car. The boys, seven and five years old, had a hard time sitting still when we started across the Appalachians. They bounced on the back seat getting Coochie riled up and barking. For them, the trip was an adventure. For me, it might well be a rescue mission.

"Lookit," Archie said. "Is that a bear?"

I didn't see a bear, but Coochie must have smelled one because she growled protection for her family. The dog had settled in nicely with the boys, even sleeping at the foot of George's bed one night, Archie's the next.

"That's no bear," George announced. "It's a monster coming to eat you up!"

"Aw," Archie said. "Ain't no such thing."

"Don't say ain't, Archie," Dottie tossed out.

Thankfully, when we passed the mountains and reached the plains, both boys and dog fell asleep. After a few hours, Dottie took the wheel, a less confident driver than my sister—and slower, too. When they woke from their naps, the boys ate peanut butter sandwiches and munched apples, tossing the cores out the window for scavengers. There wasn't much traffic, but we weren't in a rush—precious cargo.

A cold wind blew into the car and I told the boys to roll up the windows, forgetting Coochie needed a bath.

"Pee-yew," Archie complained.

"Okay, but don't roll them down more than an inch," I corrected.

The dog odor was mild compared to what hit us when we finally reached Saint Louis. What I hadn't seen the last time I was in the city was a camp of shanty dwellings set along the Mississippi River, a tumbledown town that ran for most of a mile along the river's banks.

"What in heaven's name?" Dottie said.

"It stinks," George said.

He was right—it stank of rotting food scraps, smoke, and sewage—distinctly shit and piss.

"Slow down, Dottie," I said. "And keep your eyes peeled." I didn't mention Willie. Heaven forbid we find her by the piles of trash drooping in front of the hovels. Beyond the shacks, more trash floated on the river.

"For crying out loud," George said. "What is it?"

"It's a Hooverville," I said in a whisper.

"A what?"

How could I explain to my young men what they were seeing? I could barely believe it myself.

"These are hardworking people who've lost their jobs," I said. "And if you lose your job, you lose your house. And what do you and your children do then?"

"What'd they lose their jobs for? Are they crooks?" Archie asked.

"Times have been hard, son."

George perched on the edge of the seat examining the settlement. "Looks like they found cardboard, tin, and, and—"

"Tarpaper," Dottie said, scrunching up her nose.

"There's some lumber nailed together," I said, "and what looks like orange crates."

A horde of grimy children played in the street or squatted like little rats in the makeshift doorway of a poor excuse for a dwelling.

"Must be thousands of people living here," Dottie said. "Bless their hearts."

"They look hungry, Daddy," Archie said. We passed a truck handing out quarts of milk, but the residents of shantytown had hollow cheeks, their faces sad looking. A woman swept the floor of her shack as small children played around her feet.

"How long they gotta live here?" George asked.

"I don't know," I said. "I guess it's up to President Roosevelt. They've been here since Hoover was president. Probably five years."

"That must be why they call this place Hooverville," Dottie said.

"Was Mr. Hoover a bad man?" Archie asked.

"I reckon you could say that," I said.

Dottie took out a handkerchief and covered her nose. "There must be all manner of diseases. I mean, where do they bathe? Hygiene has to be a problem."

"Roll the windows up," I said. But even through the glass I heard yelling, children crying. In other places, groups of men sat on buckets or wobbly chairs and strummed guitars. Hands clapped and someone beat a rhythm on the bottom of an upturned barrel. Sure they looked hungry—but not unhappy. That said something about human nature. No matter how deprived the situation, there was always a way to raise spirits and hope for something better.

"Take a good look, boys," I said, "and remember how lucky you are." I was pretty lucky myself to keep my job at the sawmill. Dottie had a jar she kept money in saying she didn't trust banks. She was right—if we'd had our money in a bank account in 1929, we'd have lost it all like some folks in town. I wondered about Willie. She'd had some good luck—except for a few stays in prison. I was afraid her luck had run out.

Coochie had her nose in the air. Either she smelled something familiar or she had a sense. I wished I could read her mind.

It was getting on to late afternoon, and I turned the car up toward Midtown and tried to recall where Willie's boarding house was. When I saw a familiar neighborhood, I found McPherson Avenue through a gray haze. Streetlights were on in the middle of the day and I could hardly breathe the air.

"People must be burning coal to stay warm," Dottie said. "It smells like our house in Silver Ridge in the winter." The handkerchief came again to her nose. "Lord—I'll take wood smoke any day."

I found the address, a two-story brick rowhouse. When I knocked on the door, an elderly woman opened and asked what I wanted.

"I'd like to speak with Willie Carter Sharpe," I said.

"Who?" She wore a drab, baggy dress, her hair pulled into a tight bun.

"Wilhelmina Collins?" I tried.

"Sorry." The woman shook her head.

Willie had probably signed on with some made up name. But the trial had been in papers across the country, and by now the landlady would have discovered my sister's identity. Every state in America—probably every country in the world—dealt in bootleg liquor.

"The lady I believe you're looking for no longer lives here," the woman said.

Willie hadn't written me about moving. She'd have given me a new address if she had one.

"Do you know where she's staying?"

"I wish I did," the woman snapped. "She's behind in the rent. Three months' worth, in fact." She scowled at me. "I don't run a charity operation, you know."

"So you put her out on the street?"

"There were renters with cash waiting for a room. I didn't have a choice."

Since she wasn't driving, Willie must have run out of money. I turned away without thanking the old hag. How she could put Willie out in times like these was unforgivable. Willie must still have been in the city. Where else could she have gone?

Dusk was falling, and the boys were hungry. I'd seen a diner across the railroad tracks where we might be able to get plates of spaghetti to fill their empty bellies. Right as we got to the tracks, the arms came down and bells rang announcing a train approaching. A train—especially a freight train—always generated glee with my young men. Archie jumped when the locomotive blasted its loud whistle, and I told them to get ready to count the cars.

Coming from our left, the train was nearly to the crossing, its bright headlamp lighting up the track. I looked to the right and spotted three people walking beside the tracks, two young boys carrying what appeared to be pillowcases and a woman with a large basket on her hip.

"Here it comes," the woman yelled to the boys. "Keep watch, now."

By this time, they were not more than shadows. Something told me to pull the car to the side. I got out and ordered my family to stay put.

When the train reached the crossing, I saw the cars were loaded above the brim with black coal. Beside the rattling string of metal, the three strangers stood dangerously close as the train chugged past, dropping chunks of coal. The boys, who looked near my son's ages, had skin so dark they were almost invisible as night fell around them.

Over the rattle of the metal wheels on metal rails, the woman hollered, "Pick it up, now. Don't miss any. That there's black gold."

The boys dashed along the moving train gathering coal into their bags, and the woman bent to pick up lumps for her basket.

Finally, when the train passed, I heard the smaller boy say, "What we gonna do with all this coal, Willie?"

"Some pay good money for coal these days," she said. "And good money means these chunks gonna feed us, Theo, that's what."

"You eatin' coal?" the bigger boy said. "Must be hard up."

"Me? Naw, I got Italian leather on my feet and diamonds in my teeth."

The boy tilted his head toward her feet. "Look to me like you wearing boots."

She was so thin I hardly recognized her. Her hair needed washing and her dress was soiled with coal dust and dirt. I wanted to run up to her but I waited, not taking a chance of embarrassing her.

"Say, didn't you used to drive for bootleggers?" the bigger boy said.

"You must be thinking of somebody else," Willie said. "Gimme them bags now. Here's your nickels."

"Say, Willie," the boy called Theo said.

"Yeah?"

"Ma's got a stew on the burner. Come on soon."

"Sure thing, Theo."

When the youngsters ran off, I walked toward my sister.

"Willie?" I said.

She squinted at me. "What're you doing here, Jimmy?" She said it as if I'd suddenly emerged from a dream she was having.

"I've been looking for you."

"Well, looks like you found me." She set down her basket and passed a hand down the side of her dress, smoothing out wrinkles. "And ain't I a sight."

"You are a sight—for sore eyes, sister." When I reached out and hugged her, she didn't resist. She smelled gamy, like a bear in its den.

"Good to see you, brother," she said.

"You're staying at that Hooverville, aren't you?" I couldn't think where else she would live.

Her hand went to her neck, a familiar gesture. "It's not so bad," she said.

A cold wind started blowing. "You must be about frozen. Don't you have a coat, Willie?"

"Gave it to somebody who needed it more than I did."

"Look," I said, "why don't you come to Roanoke with Dottie and me and the kids? We'll put you up until you get straightened out."

She shook her head. "You know I can't go back there. I wouldn't last a day. You saw what they did to Jeff Richards, didn't you? Shot him down in cold blood before he had a chance to testify against them. And they'd come after me for revenge." Her eyes met mine. "I'm not welcome in Virginia, Jimmy."

"Then how about West Virginia? Or even better, Maryland. Stuart's gaffers wouldn't have jurisdiction there."

"I wouldn't count on that." She stepped away from me. "Don't worry about me—I can manage here."

"Then let me give you money. I have some saved." Dottie would not be too happy, but Willie was my closest kin. When Pop gave up the farm and moved in with us, he didn't last long, as I expected. The undertaker said he died of a broken heart. Willie was all the family I had left. I was willing to give her anything I had.

"I don't take handouts," she said.

My heart was racing. What was I supposed to do, leave her like that without knowing what would become of her?

"At least come have supper with us. We're going to a diner up the road a ways. You look like you could use a hot meal."

She shook her head. "I'm staying with Theo and his ma. They're expecting me."

I was getting exasperated. No matter what her circumstances, my older sister was still calling the shots.

"Expecting you in one of those—shacks?"

Willie dipped her head toward the river. "We call it Merrytown. We all make the best of it, Jimmy. Some people look down on us, but a third of the population here have lost everything. We're making do together."

A lump formed in my throat. Willie was down and out, and she didn't want help from me. I'd never felt more helpless.

"They're good folks, Jimmy. They take care of me and I care for them, whites and Negroes alike."

I had trouble getting words out. A few seconds passed, neither of us able to speak. Finally, I said, "Let me give you a lift. You can squeeze in." I looked at her haul of coal. "We'll put your stuff in the trunk."

My sons were holding the dog by the collar. Coochie was barking and struggling to get away, lunging toward the car window.

"Who've you got there?" Willie asked.

"Let her go, boys," I yelled.

In seconds Coochie was out of the car and running up to Willie. She stooped to the dog.

"Coochie, you rascal," she said, her eyes welling up. Paws on Willie's shoulders, Coochie licked the salty tracks on her cheeks. "Never thought I'd see you again, girl," she whispered, her voice hoarse with regret and gratitude at the same time. She looked up at me and a sob escaped her. Her life had been so much harder than mine. Now she deserved this one good thing.

"You take her," I said. The boys' hearts would be broken, but my sister's heart needed healing. Coochie was good medicine.

Willie nodded. "It's not far," she said. "We can walk from here." She leaned forward and kissed my cheek. "You be good now, Junebug." Then she picked up her basket and spoke to the dog. "C'mon, Coochie."

Coochie took a long look at the car where my sons waited, then at me.

"It's okay, Coochie," I said.

Slowly Coochie turned toward my sister. Her tail wagged, and she bounded toward Willie, heeling beside her as they walked along the tracks. It was the last time I'd see either of them.

Afterword

After the 1935 Great Moonshine Conspiracy trial in which twenty of the accused men were found guilty, three were acquitted, and eleven did not contest the allegations, Willie Carter Sharpe left Franklin County to live out her life in anonymity. It is suspected she returned to Saint Louis. Reports of seeing her in Maryland were rumors that were never substantiated. Some say she died in 1970 at age 67, but no obituary or grave was ever found. As far as is known, Willie never got behind the wheel of a car again.

Willie's reputation has resonated around the world. Songs have been composed about her and in Montpelier, France, a cocktail bar bears her name.

T. Keister Greer in his book *The Great Moonshine Conspiracy Trial of 1935* noted that in 1945 the original transcript of the trial was wired to the clerk of the U.S. District Court in Harrisonburg and then, Greer wrote, "It simply disappeared from the face of the earth." The trial lasted ten weeks after which the jury took three days to return guilty verdicts against all defendants except the two deputy sheriffs and the Virginia Commonwealth's Attorney.

In 1946 a federal grand jury indicted two dozen people on charges of tampering with the jury, and twenty-two defendants were convicted. The file in that case also has disappeared. As for the murder of Thomas Jefferson Richards, two brothers were convicted of the crime, but Greer said he believed the missing trial transcript might contain evidence that the brothers were innocent.

The only written trial records left in existence are accounts in Franklin County's daily newspapers and articles in *The Roanoke Times*.

Acknowledgments

Because my people are from Southwest Virginia, for many years I've been fascinated with the bootleg liquor business. I've written about Willie Carter Sharpe in my family memoir, *Hot Springs and Moonshine Liquor* and in an essay titled "Rum Running Queen" published in the anthology *Southern Sin: True Stories of the Sultry South and Women Behaving Badly* (Creative Nonfiction Foundation 2014). Summer visits to aunts, uncles, and cousins in Roanoke, Covington, Buchanan, Christiansburg, and Potts Creek were a regular occurrence. My relatives have fed me, prayed over me, taken me to their churches, and told me stories that have stayed with me. For decades my family has owned a cabin on Jennings Creek just yards from the Appalachian Trail in Arcadia, Virginia, in the heart of the Blue Ridge Mountains. The people in Southwest Virginia are the best folks I've ever known.

Greer's book *The Great Moonshine Conspiracy Trial of 1934* was extremely helpful in recreating the courtroom scenes in this novel. *Spirits of Just Men* by Charles D. Thompson, Jr. and *The Wettest County in the World* by Matt Bondurant helped me capture the Virginia Prohibition landscape and spirit.

In writing this novel, I'm grateful for the careful eyes of members of my writing group, including Sally Baldwin, Ann Moreau Kensek, Carol Talmage, Jacquelyn Tuxill, Tom Verner, and Jacqueline Weyrauch. Thanks to my brother Don Vanness and his wife Monte for offering me a taste of Franklin County moonshine whiskey purchased from a student working his way through Ferrum College where their daughter Kimberly was also a student. And mountains of thanks to my publisher Reagan Rothe and the crew at Black Rose Writing for believing in my work.

Finally, I'm eternally grateful to you, my readers, who are patient enough to read this novel, as well as my other books, and who are generous in leaving reviews. If it weren't for you, I'd have no reason to set pen to paper. Thank you.

About the Author

Louella Bryant is the author of nine books of fiction, memoir, and biography. Her award-winning writing has appeared in magazines and anthologies. A graduate of George Washington University and Vermont College of Fine Arts, Louella is a former professor of creative writing at Spalding University. Currently Louella blogs, directs a writing group, and works as an independent editor from her home in Vermont. Originally from the south, when Louella married a New Englander, she brought her sweet tooth with her. Now she pours Vermont maple syrup over pretty much everything, but she still likes to "bless your heart." Visit her website at www.louellabryant.com.

Other Titles by Louella Bryant

Note from Louella Bryant

Word-of-mouth is crucial for any author to succeed. If you enjoyed *Willie – Rum Running Queen,* please leave a review online – anywhere you are able. Even if it's just a sentence or two. It would make all the difference and would be very much appreciated.

Thanks!
Louella Bryant